# DEFCON

MICHELE PACKARD

*Recent Editorial Reviews:*

**TELLER:** *... Packard, an award-winning author writes narratives that are void of fluff and superfluous details. She shares James Patterson's view of only providing details when they serve a real purpose...The author's knowledge of the US and world history, places, customs, and traditions are truly amazing. Teller succeeds as a rocket-fast read that is both a great work of Science Fiction speculation and a hard-boiled detective story. It sparkles with its eccentric characters and a clever, twisty plot that culminates with a satisfying conclusion..."*
— AuthorsReading.com

*...The novel is very well written for this genre. It's engaging, fun, hilarious, and pretty easy to follow. Packard does a great job weaving in perfectly relevant pop culture references to increase accessibility and relevancy. The story might have been a bit big for how much territory Matti covered in these few pages, but it definitely worked for a page turning plot. All in all, Matti is a fantastic character who was obviously worth a trilogy. Her narration and humor work very well, especially mixed in with her courageous and tough nature..."*
—Writers Digest

**COUNTERINTELLIGENCE:** *... The more the reader delves into this fascinating read, he will wonder if fiction is becoming factual. Or is Packard such an astute intellectual and researcher that she is able to expose reality through the use of fiction? With several intense thrillers to her credit, this award-winning author of action-packed contemporary fiction is a name to watch.* – AuthorsReading.com

*Counterintelligence is one of the year's top political thrillers.*
— BestThrillers.com

**DEFCON:** ... *Prior fans of genetically enhanced superwoman Matti Baker will welcome her return in Defcon, while newcomers will easily fall into her world. This is because Matti employs a feisty voice in describing an encounter which once again tests her ability to survive, protect her family, and prove effective in her efforts to thwart the bad guys and support everything she loves... The challenge lies in what label to assign Defcon, because it doesn't fit neatly into any pat genre read. Military in nature, but with a psychological force that lends it a deep personal flavor; thriller in action, but tempered by family relationships and close friendships; and flavored by political and historical information that invite debate and thought, Defcon is quite simply a standout for its adventure, tone, and powerful, driven female protagonists.*

— D. Donovan, Donovan Literary Services

### Readers Reviews:

*"In Counterintelligence, author Michele Packard does an amazing job of sending Matti Baker, a fictional bad-ass-female character, in to take care of everything wrong with the world today. If only she were real!! Matti is a cross between Ryan Reynolds in the "Adam Project" and Halle Berry in "John Wick III". If Ryan Reynold's snarky throw away lines and Halle Berry's kick-ass assassin moves aren't enough to hook you, throw in movie and song references along with her impeccable taste and she puts James Bond to shame. I'd say Matti Baker is the perfect character for a Feature Film or TV Series. I hear some of that Will Smith money is freed up...get to it Hollywood!*

*"The plot was so interesting and the character of Matti so much fun, I literally could not put the book down until I finished. Matti and Bethany are like Charlie's Angels, only with intelligence. LOL. Matti actually reminds me of the bride in the films Kill Bill. Badass to the nth degree and focused on getting what needs to be done. A well-executed edge-of-your-seat story."*

*"Your dry wit and humor had me laughing out loud. Which is interesting when sitting in a public place and reading your book. The writing is gritty, intense and pulled me right in. However, what I liked about your writing is that it isn't just action scenes with succinct writing. It's also emotional which helps round out Matti and keeps her from being one-dimensional."*

*"Packard continues to entertain but also educate as so many of her books have so many current issues!! I look forward to what comes next from this brilliant author!!"*

*"Wow, Michele Packard had me at the opening sentence and didn't let go. The 4th in the Matti Baker series does not disappoint. Song and movie quotes accompany this wild ride of terrorism, suspense, and hilarity - yeah, you heard me right. Packard's talent for capturing the current state of affairs in fiction (is it really?) in a well-told story is unparalleled."*

*"All American badass Matti Baker is back with a vengeance in this fast-paced political thriller."*

*"DEFCON is a non-stop thrill ride. Once you pick this book up, don't make other plans because you won't put it down until the end. Five stars."*

*"Did someone leave the stove on? Matti's baking the competition and we're all gonna take a bite."*

*"I loved it!"*

*"CAN'T WAIT for the next one!"*

*"Just finished DEFCON and thought it was excellent!"*

# ACKNOWLEDGEMENTS

To O.O. Wilson
A POW & Bataan Death March Survivor
My Grandfather
&
William J. Hosmer (HOZ)
The real deal Thunderbird

*To every reader who purchases:*
*Thank you for your support and hope you enjoy the adventures.*

*Carpe diem*

Follow for more information and insights:
**www.michelepackard.com**
**Instagram: @aesopstories**

First Printing 2023

ISBN: 979-8-9876077-0-1 Paperback
ISBN: 979-8-9876077-1-8 Hardback

Cover & Book formatting by Platform House
www.platformhousepublishing.com

# MAIN CHARACTERS:

**MATTI BAKER** – Genetically created with the collusion between seven scientists. She is a female triplet with two brothers. Number one contract operative of the US. Her genetic key is coveted with sinister consequences. Scientists have been unsuccessful in replicating. She is the genesis of it all. (If you don't figure this out by end of this story…)

**TOM** – Matti's beloved husband. Former franchise owner, now serving in special operations to assist Matti and fellow colleagues. Watches Bachelorette (to Matti's repugnance).

**BETHANY** – Matti's dearest and best friend since training academy. Don't call her Number Two without serious repercussions. She is the Yin to Matti's Yang.

**FREDDY** – Matti's previous commander and formerly believed to be her biological father. Just goes to show, you don't have to be blood to be family.

**JAKE** – Former Navy Seal, now chairs training program for elite operatives.

**STEVE** – Best friend of Jake and former Navy Seal, who co-chairs training program.

**BESSUM** – Head of the Albanian mob and close confidant of Matti.

**LILY** – Cousin of Bessum, head of the Sicilian mob, and close confidant of Matti.

Last, but not least:

**MATTHEW, MARY, MARK** – Matti's and Tom's triplet children, whom she will defend at ALL costs, and has killed to protect.

**OTHER CHARACTERS:**

**DAVID** – One of Matti's triplet brothers. His wife is Marie; they have two beautiful daughters, Chanlor and Ryan.

**RENAT** – Also goes by Jardani. Matti's other triplet brother. No known relatives.

**JEFF & KELLY** – Kelly is the sister to Matti's biological mother. She and her husband became the adoptive parents to Matti at birth.

**TIA** – brought in by the 'agency' to train Matti in youth. Now assists with protection of Jeff & Kelly.

**ALDO** – Head of the High Camorra. Has relations with TIA.

**BORRELLI** – President of the United States.

**INTRATOR** – Vice President of the United States.

**SEDLIN** – Director of CIA, in need of a companion.

**LONG** – Deputy Director of CIA for Operations, may become Sedlin's companion one day.

**AINSWORTH** – Former Marine, assists with training program in Jake/Steve's absence and with special assignments.

**LARKIN** – Former Marine, friend of Ainsworth, and assists with special covert assignments.

**JACKSON**– Newest member to entourage. Romance writer and political activist.

# PRELUDE

---

*A house divided against itself cannot stand.*
*— Abraham Lincoln*

*Our struggle is not against flesh and blood, but against the rulers,*
*against the authorities, against the powers of this dark world and*
*against the spiritual forces of evil in the heavenly realms.*
*— Ephesians 6:12*

A SOLDIER'S MINUTE IN BATTLE IS ALL YOU GET. You get one minute of everything at once and one minute before it is nothing. I had just under 400 meters to determine who had been shot. Was it my husband or one of my best friends?

Usain Bolt was twenty-two years old when he was recorded running twenty-three miles per hour. I was making him look like a rookie in my supernaturally enhanced state as I ran towards the entrance to confront my fears.

In 1959, North American Aerospace and Defense Command (NORAD) created a national government emergency measurement and alertness scale based on the Cuban Missile Crisis. (Level I is the worst case (nuclear attack). Level V is the best case.) In fact, at that time, the US reached level II. As of right now, we are on level III. The US has never reached Level I. Yet. It surely would be the sign of tribulation if it does.

| CONDITION | DEFCON I | DEFCON II | DEFCON III | DEFCON IV | DEFCON V |
|---|---|---|---|---|---|
| ↓ | ↓ | ↓ | ↓ | ↓ | ↓ |
| EXCERCISE TERM | COCKED PISTOL | FAST PACE | ROUND HOUSE | DOUBLE TAKE | FADE OUT |
| READINESS | MAXIMUM READINESS | ARMED FORCES: 6 HRS OR LESS TO DEPLOY & ENGAGE | MAXIMUM AIR FORCE: 15 MINUTES TO MOBILIZATION | ABOVE NORMAL | NORMAL |
| DESCRIPTION | NUCLEAR WAR IMMINENT | NEAR NUCLEAR WAR | FORCE READINESS INCREASED ABOVE NORMAL LEVELS | INTEL WATCH INCREASED SECURITY MEASURES STRENGTHENED | LOWEST STATE |

I always operate on level III (despite the scale only measuring nuclear threats). We can discuss (argue) all day long that any Tom, Dick, and Harry could possess weapons of mass destruction, so theoretically it may be time to update this scale with additional parameters.

Being a genetically manufactured "experiment" of our government that had gone awry, I was the sole female with two other biological brothers. Not to be condescending, but that would mean we were born triplets. *(For the love of God, don't make me explain how we are not identical).* We were separated at birth and have never crossed paths. I have three children and can confirm at least one other child by my brother, so a new little CRISPR nation of mutating individuals is developing.

For over twenty-five years, I have been contracted by the same US government that created me to identify, locate and *neutralize* individuals and countries that pose a threat to the United States. Understand: the key word is neutralize. Not to toot my own horn, but there's a reason they contact me when they want to get the job done.

My direct team consisted of my de-facto commander and wanna-be father (Freddy), my best friend (Bethany), and two retired Navy Seals (Jake and Steve. Sidenote: Bethany was shacking up with Steve…), two European mafia mercenaries (Bessum and Lily) and my darling husband (Tom). One might say, we are an eclectic bunch.

We had just concluded our last mission that resulted in the acting-President taking her own life when it was revealed that she colluded with other countries and internal agencies, attempted to assassinate the President and Vice President, manufactured and mass distributed a deadly virus that killed millions worldwide, harbored terrorists, committed federal conspiracy and cybercrimes… *I really wanted to put that bullet in her thick head myself. Oh, well.*

I alone possess vials that other individuals and nations want. These vials are the genetic make-up of my manufactured man-made creation. Their motives to reacquire these vials were to (1) conceal, (2) manufacture for weapons of mass destruction, (3) or use them as an antidote. My bet was on option #2. Genocide, New World Order, whatever you want to name it. *Hasta la vista, baby.*

My team was together at our compound in Colorado. The 'boys' were entering the front entrance after successfully retrieving the daughter of one of my unidentified brothers. *(My niece. Keep up here).*

My two military trained German Shepherds first heard the two shots as they spliced the air. Bethany ran towards the firepower we had set-up on the property. I ran toward the intended recipients.

I was now operating at DEFCON II.

Billie Eilish's *No Time to Die, was* pounding through my head as I sprinted.... *Faces from my past return, Another lesson yet to learn, That I'd fallen for a lie, You were never on my side...*

I quickly changed directions with my own version of Thomas Shelby from *Peaky Blinders...*

*"It's not a good ideal to look at Matti Baker the wrong way."*

# ONE

THE FRONT ENTRANCE TO OUR COMPOUND consisted of two large stone column walls with double-gated wrought iron doors that swung out to the two-lane deserted country road. Huge evergreen trees adorn the long curving driveway bordered by a split rail fence, providing picturesque beauty while maintaining absolute privacy.

I was thirty yards out and counting, but saw nothing. I could hear and feel the rapid-fire ammunition, producing a thunderous, rippling effect and only hoped that Bethany had successfully taken out any culprit(s). Otherwise, I could be the next victim.

The M134 minigun was originally designed to be mounted on helicopters boasting a fire rate of up to six thousand rounds per minute. It simulates a laser show. It's pure destruction. We had two mounted just at the base of our compound, and by all accounts, Bethany intended to fire until they were empty. Additional noise was now escalating as she traversed the landscape of the snow-massed mountains, coming down like an avalanche.

The shadow of a bald eagle soaring high above was projected on the driveway ahead of me, as almost guiding me to the scene. I ran even faster. The dogs were scouring the terrain on a hunt for anything that moved watching every move of the eagle. I was at max speed when I arrived just short of the gate. 3-2-1. Nothing. *WTF.*

The eagle took off in the other direction.

I already had my Heckler & Koch HK45T out, attempting to sight any and everything. I wasn't aiming to maim. I was going to unload just as Bethany was. I slowly approached the gate, checking my back, when two people popped up on both sides of the stone wall screaming, "Matti, don't shoot!"

Milliseconds. That's all it takes to compute. Relief flooded me as I saw my husband, Tom, and then I saw Steve. I was vacillating between smiling to understanding that someone else's demise would most likely be imminent. It had to be Jake and/or my niece Chanlor that may have fallen victim. Snipers are trained to shoot twice. To ensure death.

My dogs, Koda and Bruiser, were now motionless in a hunched attack mode. Slowly, I noticed a figure protruding over the column wall. Another visible sigh emitted from my body when I saw it was Jake. My immediate and extended family was still intact. Pulling her up by arm, Jake raised Chanlor. She looked ghostly white. I immediately did a one-eighty with my pistol ready to fire for any intruders as this didn't compute. Whoever was sent to shoot wouldn't miss. The dogs circled back searching but came up with nothing.

When all was cleared, I slowly walked backwards to the column walls to join them. "What the hell happened? And how did they miss?"

Before my husband Tom could even respond, Jake interrupted. "I've never seen anything like this in my entire career. It's nothing short of divine intervention."

The thundering fire power from Bethany had vanished. The silence was now deafening.

Everyone's face showed incredulous disbelief of what had just transpired. I then witnessed that Steve had blood slowly trickling from his collarbone. "How bad?" I directed to him.

"I'll be ok. No artery. It went through and through, but I will need additional med attention," Steve explained.

Tom embraced me as I grabbed his radio and relayed to Bethany. "B, No casualties here. Confirm target acquired."

"Oh, Stevie Nicks has nothing on me. I landslided that Mofo. Whoever it was is now one with nature until Spring when it thaws."

"We'll be up there in ten. Get the backhoe out. We need to find out who it was and who sent them."

"Are you kidding? It will take all day to do that with what I unloaded."

"Should have thought about that beforehand. And...FYI. When it involves snow, it's an avalanche, not a landslide."

"Potatoe, potato."

All were still in a fog as we headed back to make our way to the compound. No one said a word while we journeyed back. I had Butthole Surfers's *Pepper* ringing through my head...*Well, it should have been a better shot, and got him in the head, They were all in love with dyin', they were drinkin' from a fountain that was pourin' like an avalanche comin' down the mountain...*

Freddy had our med kit ready for Steve's arrival. Steve generally was our medic on missions, so he self-administered first aid while Bethany looked on, fuming. You didn't want to mess with her when she was pissed.

Tom was giving me silent glances, shaking his head ever so slightly to signal "wait till you hear this." We gathered in the makeshift sit room to debrief what had just gone down.

"Jake, let's start from the top. Everything you can think of. Don't leave out any details."

"Steve, Chan and I were pulling up the front gate when we saw Tom approaching on his ATV. We got out of the car before the gate entrance, walked over to where Tom had stopped to admire and check out the new toy, and were walking around it as he pointed out the extra features. Nice ride by the way…Now, this is the part that you won't believe. As we are chatting it up, we see a bald eagle soaring overhead, circling. It was massive. Wingspan over 7 feet. We look at it in admiration and go on about our talking. But you could tell, it had its sights on something. We don't think anything about it figuring it's homing in on dinner. Next thing you know, it comes barreling down, and you could physically feel the "whoosh," as we think, it's targeting us. Steve shoves Chan out of the way, throwing her to the ground as it's coming right for us. It then proceeds to circle us, causing a vortex; dust flying up everywhere. We couldn't see. I swear to Christ, I thought this was a scene from the movie, *The Birds*. Then, poof. This mammoth eagle changes direction again, at what felt like supersonic speeds, towards the compound. I've never witnessed anything so fast. We scrambled to the take coverage to the column wall while I was booking it to get my rifle. Fuck, man, it felt like I was back on deployment. Steve announced he was hit. We're still thinking it's from the deranged eagle, until we also see a bullet mark in the gate, with a puff of smoke. Next thing we heard was firing on the ridge line while we took cover and were waiting it out to figure out what the hell was happening."

Tom and Steve were now chiming in collectively in a heightened state, overlapping each other confirming the same story. Chanlor hadn't moved or said a word. She was noticeably in shock.

I already knew the answer but had to ask for verification. "So, now that you know a shooter was involved, who do you think the intended target or targets were?"

Jake and Steve looked at each other before answering. Jake looked at me and confirmed my suspicions. "It was intended for Chanlor."

I sent a quick text on my phone.

We had come full circle with this chick. The verdict was still out for me, but the others had come to accept her. Not on our radar, we originally met her in Vail where she mickied my dear friend Doug with an explosive charge that killed him. She also did the same to Jake, but we were able to dislodge in the knick of time. Once she was under our custody, we realized she hadn't had an option, as the then-acting-FDA Commissioner, Roman Wagner, was using her and her company to fast-track an approval process on a new vaccine. *May he rest in peace, that douche bag.* They also put her mother in an assisted nursing home. The mother would never recover from the injuries she sustained.

It wasn't until we had Chanlor and Wagner in interrogations that bloodwork confirmed that she and I shared DNA strands; confirming she was an offspring of one of my brothers that I have yet to meet. Despite trying to take his life, Jake took a fondness to her that I'm still unable to comprehend. *He really needs a psyche eval.*

Bethany looked over to me. She was still fuming that Steve got hit, but was relieved that it was minor. Freddy had been quiet.

Almost too quiet. For a man to be in this line of high-level work this long and not commenting was unnerving.

Finally, Freddy piped up, "What do you think, Matti?"

"I think there are signs everywhere. Eagles are listed twenty-eight times in the Bible, and they are often depicted as the resurrection in Christian art. They can be a symbol of loyalty, strength, devotion, and freedom. Many claim that if you see one flying over your head, it's a sign you're on the right path. Let's hope that we are."

All just sat there stone-faced.

"So much for the teaching lesson," I feigned. "I think they targeted Chanlor because they want to eliminate our genetic DNA make-up. It looks like they want to conceal versus replicate. So, there's a possibility I was wrong in my initial assumption. Therefore, they will be targeting me, as well."

Tom turned to me worried. "What about the kids?"

"I already notified Ainsworth to move them ASAP. That's who I texted earlier. They'll be going to Area 51, but we need to make some pit stops first. Freddy, take Steve to get his collarbone stitched up by our favorite doctor. Jake, prepare provisions for our trip and get the plane prepped. Tom, contact Bes and Lily and fill them in. Chanlor, how about you just stay here and try to relax? *Good lord.* Bethany, let's start digging."

"You've got to be kidding me!" she said, exasperated.

"Do I look like I'm kidding? This isn't a Reacher movie where they just move on never asking why or who. We need to find out who they sent. That will tell us who is targeting us. Everyone: we don't have time to spare. Let's get on it and plan to meet at Nola's.

For trained professionals, you could hear them all bitching and mumbling under their breaths as they walked out. I could hear Steve asking Tom, "Did she just admit she was wrong? And how the hell does she know eagles are listed twenty-eight times in the Bible, off the top of her head?"

Tom didn't look back. In a whispered and hushed tone, he responded, "Dude, trust me. I've never known her to be wrong, and she just knows."

# TWO

BETHANY HAD DONNED QUITE THE LOOK as she got the backhoe from our utility shed. Wearing a white Ghoster Glam, one-piece softshell ski suit, you would have thought she was attending a 007 premier. With the contrast to her flawless black skin, and her hair in a wavy, high pony, she gave Halle Berry a run for her money.

"Nice look," was all I said as I gave the proverbial head nod as I walked towards the site.

"Where do you want to start?" she barked, incensed that we were doing this right now as she jumped into the driver's seat. I knew she wanted to be with Steve, but it was a flesh wound. He'd be ok. We needed to know who had been sent and was targeting us.

"I don't know…how about we used the specially trained military dogs to help trace?" I said in a direct but subtle voice.

Point taken.

I'd acquired Koda and Bruiser, my devout German Shepherds, when I was in solitude for a year, recovering from an ass beating and complete rebuilding. Unlike Humpty Dumpty, it took some time to put me back together again. Bethany took care of my family as I recuperated and planned my vengeance. I could never pay her back for what she did, and occasionally, she reminded me of that. We were best friends. We'd kill and die for one another. She was my person, my balance…but right now she was not happy.

These dogs were trained for tracking, explosive detection, and search and rescue. Koda and Bruiser were also trained to defend and attack. At times, they could be used for psychological torture. What can I say? I was alone for 12 months; we had a lot of time on our hands.

German Shepherds are a preferred breed for this line of work due their strength, loyalty, and ability to stay calm in the most hostile environments. (Unlike the other two "family" dogs that were acquired during my absence: big boned...PC for overweight... labs).

It took no time for them to navigate the general area of our dead assailant. Bethany was attacking the side of the mountain on a mission.

"Careful, B. We don't need another avalanche, and I'd prefer to cart this piece of shit out in one piece." Common fact: Avalanches in Colorado are very common. Thousands occur every year, and Colorado has the highest avalanche fatality rates of any state. I didn't want to be added to this statistic.

"A few more seconds. Get the shovels ready," she yelled over the loud noise of the motor.

Blending into the snowcapped side, a figure finally emerged. Bethany and I looked at it and then at each other with a feigned repulse. As we took the shovels to dig around, the body had collapsed with the right arm up in a futile attempt to protect the riddled, goggled face as the snow engulfed them. The jacket liner was peppered with bullet fragments, showing the violently-complete tearing and separation of the mid-section, with red, crimson blood sprayed in all directions. So much for trying to take it in one piece. We'd be hauling out in multiple piles.

Fortunately, or unfortunately, it would be a lighter load for us to carry. We were retrieving a woman.

# THREE

IT SHOULDN'T MATTER that this was a woman versus a man. Equal rights, right? Men had taken took no mercy on me as a female when they beat me to an inch of my life. We are trained for it not to make a difference; but don't kid yourself: it does. Just like when anyone was sent to war and had to shoot a child carrying C4 in their backpacks. It haunts you. Every. Damn. Day.

To add to the equation, our unidentified perp was wearing USSR army mountain sniper goggles. They have direct ventilation and don't steam up inside, and can withstand vast temperature ranges. So…we had a female, Russian operative on American soil trying to eliminate Chanlor, and potentially myself and my family.

Bethany was taking facial photos (of what was left) and printing her fingerprints to send out for any hits on recognition. I carefully dug around her and found the Dragunov semi-automatic sniper rifle that she clutched in her left hand. A rifle can't help you in an avalanche. Most people (myself included) can't pronounce correctly, Snayperskaya Vintovka Dragunova, but this is a relatively light sniper rifle, easier for a female to control. It allows rapid fire. I'm unsure why she only got off two shots before her demise.

The light pack on her back carried her additional ammo and supplies. Jackpot. There was a phone. One number. Area code 202. *Shit.*

I stared at the number, trying my best Denzel Washington attempt (in *The Bone Collector) to* connect dots and numbers together. I've seen this number. Lobbyist? Department of Defense? *Think.*

My phone rang, kicking me momentarily out of thought, as I saw that it was Freddy. "Hey, what's up?"

"Matti, get out now. Whoever this is, blew up the entire lab and staff. Doc is gone. We need to go dark. NOW."

*Doc is gone.* Doc Rihani had put me back together too many times to count over the years. He literally rebuilt me, making me a newer version of a Bionic Woman. He was in the process of analyzing the blood of Chanlor, the kids and myself to see how this worldwide pandemic virus was mutating in each of us. Lately, I had supernatural strength and speed, and my body was freakishly repairing itself from past injuries. As an original host, it was imperative to know my genetic make-up to determine potential outcomes on my children. Similar to the global vaccine's pages of potential side-effects *(f'in pages in lengths)*, we were cross-checking and making our own list.

*Doc is gone. It's always about money. Greed. Focus.* Purdue Pharma and the Sackler family negotiated a six billion settlement for the encouragement and misleading marketing on breakthrough occurrences. Six billion. The current vaccine manufacturers were marketing breakthrough infections and additional boosters needed now even for young children, despite the science of it all. The CDC had proposed another twenty-two-billion-dollar budget. A virus needs a host to survive. *(The fact that several FDA and the NAID Directors are on the Board of Director's for the same pharm companies that they passed legislation for is coincidental, right? Jesus Christ.)*

Society worldwide was mutating as a result of years now under the strain of this virus. Facing prolonged isolation coupled with the absence of normal, comforting things, the US government was attempting to provide a single solution for everyone here in the States. Some referred to it as mass formation psychosis. If you try to protect humanity at all costs, you don't have the opportunity to develop. Hell, even the movie *The Eternals* knew that. When you reject truth, you create confusion and chaos and, more importantly, you create dependence.

"Take Steve to UC Health in Uptown. Meet at Nola's in two hours. We'll depart separately from there."

I sent out an alert to all to prep to leave ASAP. I called Ainsworth to check on status of the kid's transport. Ainsworth was currently in charge of the kid's training program, while Jake and Steve were assisting in this current crisis. The triplets were in a class of twenty and were kicking everyone's butt - #proudmommy.

"All good, no issues. They were pissed they had to leave without a goodbye, so have fun with that. They are all racked out, right now. Mark is drooling on himself; it's pretty funny. Of course, I've already had to rotate them on front seat, as they are all bitching about who gets to sit where. Good thing they are your kids, or I'd bitch slap them back in time. Next time, I won't take the Dodge, but this was the only one fully converted to withstand any direct hits." Although I trusted Ainsworth with my kids' lives, I pictured him having grandiose ideas of being the *Last Action Hero* driving the Dodge prototype in *The Wraith*. "Get them up to Larkin safely. And, Tripp, I don't have to tell you…"

"Yeah, I know. No worries. Shoot to kill and then shoot again."

"Yep, that too."

I returned to Bethany, who was contemplating dumping Mystery Lady into a trash receptacle. "B, put a rush on it. We need to roll. Call out for a cleaner."

"We got what we need. I say we leave her. I don't think this is what they meant when they say, 'Don't feed the bears.'"

*Sweet Jesus we all need help.*

Sarah McLaughlin, *Possession*, played through my mind…*Just close your eyes dear, Into this night I wander, It's morning that I dread, Another day of knowing of The path I fear to tread…*

# FOUR

THE OFFICE OF THE Director of National Intelligence releases an annual threat assessment of the US intelligence community. The report is provided to the congressional intelligence committees in addition to the Armed Services of the House of Representatives and the Senate. Just for grins to consider: knowing our information is hacked on basically every level, how stupid must we be to provide our "playbook" to every country, or known enemy out there? Luckily, this is the stuff they are required to release publicly, i.e. – China's push for global power on cybercrimes are up significantly *(no shit)*. Just saying.

Ainsworth and Larkin had seven scientists detained in Groom Lake, aka Area 51. Larkin was brought on to oversee the captured scientists when we pulled Ainsworth to lead the training program. Both are retired Marine Sergeants, and the two of them were known to drink Jameson into the wee hours and shoot first, ask second. I liked that about them.

The seven scientists were not the original founders of my genetic creation, but were thought to be the ones trying to (unsuccessfully) duplicate it. We had two scientists from China, two from Russia, one from Middle East, one from the US, and one from Mexico.

Area 51 was originally purchased for experimental aircraft and weapons. Lockheed Martin produced the Blackbird SR-71, the fastest long-range, high altitude, Mach three plus plane ever designed. "Allegedly," test flights of this aircraft over Nevada Base were confused with UFO sightings and it was "pure" coincidence that the world's fastest airplane was decommissioned for political reasons shortly after.

So, let's skim over a few of the published nuggets from just these countries that have a collective motivation: *Greed.*

First, we have China's push for global power, with its emphasis on weapons of mass destruction and their exceeding US capabilities in space to gain in military and economic and prestige. Their increasing cooperation with Russia includes both on the defense and economic sides. *Enemy of my enemy.* China's cyber-espionage maneuvers have infiltrated the largest telecom and broadband providers providing extensive opportunities for intelligence collection, attack, and influence. They are suppressing the US web content infrastructure of anything that is viewed as threatening to its control and authoritarianism. Simply put, China's agenda is to change global norms. That ol' Belt and Road initiative alone where they are targeting worldwide infrastructure via land and maritime, makes the monopoly of Amazon looks like child's play. GREED.

Next, Mother Russia. Our nemesis of any movie from 1980s is taking on a new approach. They will continue to undermine US influence to shape global events as a major player in a new "multipolar international order," meaning they want to be one of the three kings and will stop at nothing short. Russia continues to target our infrastructure including underwater cables and industrial control. Refer to maritime under China. And let's not kid ourselves:

we KNOW Russia had influences over US elections and outcomes in the past three elections… GREED.

Our pals in the Middle East, especially Iran, are aggressively going after cybersecurity in US and allied nations. The recirculating of disinformation and anti-US content is at an all-time high. The conflicts and instability throughout Afghanistan, India-Pakistan, and a few more "stans" pose threats to US personnel and interests for coming years. Iran is developing networks inside the US with increasingly high attacks on US interests and the Homeland. ISIS and al-Qa'ida remain the greatest terrorists' threats to US interests overseas. GREED.

Our neighbors to the direct south, want to make Oxy look like tic-tacs as Mexican trafficking of fentanyl is at an all-time high. *Literally and figuratively.* Native-American's are fifty percent more likely to die of an opioid overdose than non-natives. Don't forget that fentanyl was 'allegedly' responsible for the deaths of legendary greats Prince and Tom Petty. According to the CDC, fentanyl causes half of the total number of US overdose deaths. Add in cocaine, heroin, weed and meth to round out the grocery store assortment of what they are trafficking. GREED.

We haven't even touched on US issues…or climate change, supply chain, and natural catastrophes. *Holy shit.* The lists go on. Add in unemployment and inflation and suicide has now become the newest "unspoken" pandemic.

*(This is public info. Don't fall under willed ignorance: go tap on your keyboard and search for some wisdom. For the love of God.)*

Don't confuse any of this with racism. That's what others want you to believe to confuse the issues. It's more fundamental than that.

There is one quality that is unique to the human species regardless of race, color, or gender. *It's when harm is done and or anticipated and done anyways, in response to a financial benefit...***GREED.**

In the US alone, over the last four decades, the Chief Executive Officer's pay is up one thousand three hundred and twenty-two percent (1322%), while the median worker is only up eighteen percent (18%). I love me some Peloton, but their CEO just walked out with over a hundred million for failure to perform and laid off thousands of workers in the process... *Hey, fire me!* Amazon's Jeff Bezos is making a killing off the pandemic and now can spend that five hundred million for a super-yacht. *I'm sure a reference to size can be made here.* We have golf pros playing now in the Saudi Arabia league versus playing PGA. Making two hundred million for a tour. *Ka-ching.* Disney just laid off twenty-eight thousand employees during the pandemic, but still made a two-billion-dollar profit. Gave their CEO roughly fifty million as a thank you *(which could have employed all the ones they let go. And, really, who can even afford to go to the parks now, after they continue to raise their prices?)*

Sadly, I'm a product of our society, as well, and could be viewed as just as hypocritical since I bankroll off the American government. Yes, I'm one of the highest paid private contractors of the government...*Remember why the government pays five thousand for a toilet?* I'm paid rightly so. It comes down to risk/reward/payoff, and I've neutralized threats to national and global security. Just saying...But, the majority of the money we generated was based on real estate, not income. Between selling Tom's physical fitness franchises and personal houses, we used that cashflow to make substantial investments. Economics 101 would have you invest in what people need versus want (housing, razors, ag crops). Keep that strategy for long-term growth. You want a quicker turnaround? Invest in what people desire and understand the market fluctuations and cap. (Botox, energy drinks, Tesla). Tom doesn't have a military trained background, but he put that business and psyche major to great use. *Reminder: I only harm in attempts to stop others from financially gain off of you. You're welcome.*

We no longer live in "birds of a feather" communities, with supportive friends and family to help celebrate and/or support when in need. Americans work longer hours, are now more isolated due to work-from-home options, and have fewer opportunities to develop any close relationships. We are created for connection, so we turn to the one constant connection in our life. MONEY/GREED. *God help this next generation.*

Since religion is down in the US (to only forty-four percent), I guess there's no need to add this in: *Matthew 6:12 - No one can serve two masters. For you will hate one and love the other or be devoted to one and despise the other. You cannot serve both God and money.*

So, what does this have to do with the unknown MFers trying to target 'we' who were generically created and are now mutating? Hint: It starts with G. *I think we can lay off worrying about critical race theory for the time being. How about we just start working on ANY critical thinking?*

My head hurts.

# FIVE

BACK AT OUR COMPOUND, Jake and Tom had our gear ready to go and loaded in our vehicles. *God bless them.* I was on my way to the safe to fetch the vials when I popped into Jake and Chanlor's room to check on their status.

'What's she doing?" I asked incredulously. Chanlor was on a chaise lounge and looked like she was doped up and staring off to a distant past. "Jake, we don't have time for this. Is she going to be ok?"

"She's in shock, Matti. I'm trying to rush it. She just needs some more time. She's not trained for this like we are."

"Stay here one sec," I said, and I continued to my private office and safe to fetch the vials. Moving them now was paramount and carried a significant risk, but had to be done. I returned to Jake's room and had stabbed a needle through Chanlor's neck before he knew what I was doing.

"Dammit, Matti. You've got to stop doing that."

"It had to be done. We'll get more done with her 'out' and it's easier to transport her."

"That's...like...the third time you've done that to this poor girl. She's probably not going to have any brain cells left if you keep doing that. Don't forget, she's your niece."

"She'll be fine. What I gave her is no worse than a high-dosed Ambien. And…don't forget, she is my niece." I said with a wink and as I tilted my head to indicate not to mess this up…any further.

We had the three Hummer EV's packed, and departed promptly to meet Freddy and Steve at Nola Voodoo Tavern (voted the best New Orleans-inspired bar, located in the Cole neighborhood in downtown Denver). *Damn, these are sweet vehicles.* No one would be looking for us here, as the neighborhood could get a little dicey with the upsurge in homeless in the Denver metroplex; but the red beans and rice alone was worth it. We did have a comatose Chanlor that we would be leaving in the car, but no one would see her through our blackout windows, and we had the dogs in the car, as well. We were parked behind the restaurant in the private back patio entrance and were personally carrying enough on us to take out a battalion. An additional bonus to the fabulous food and drinks Nola served was it was only ten minutes from the private airport, Travel King International, whose motto is: servicing the most discerning clientele. We ranked right up there, and had housed our Gulfstream G650ER there. *(Long story on that purchase, as Bethany bought it when I was MIA. Well, technically, I purchased it since I funded it. I know, I know…first world problems.)*

Freddy and patched-up Steve came rolling in right behind us. The owner blocked off the patio for us despite the growing crowd. Apparently, it was three-dollar mystery shot night where seven bottles were covered, and you took your pick on what you would end up with. To each his own.

"Everyone, ok? Any holdups at the hospital? I thought you might have been there before us," I asked to Steve, while Bethany was checking out his wound.

"Nah, all good. They had me in and patched up quickly. We had clearance beforehand, so there were no issues with a gunshot wound. We stuck around for a bit, as Freddy was still talking it up with the nurse who tended me."

"He what? Get out of here," I said with a disbelieving chuckle.

"NO, really, never witnessed it before. I didn't know he knew casual conversation, let alone could talk a woman up. Don't worry, I did a background check on her while they were yapping," Steve added.

"Spill it, what did she look like? What did you find on her?" Bethany inquired.

"Miss Erika is blonde, quite the looker, and is fifteen years younger than our wanna-be stud. Never been married; looks like she's worked tirelessly helping others. Only downside I could find is that she has two cats - Stray and Chloe."

"Ehh, cat lady. Stray and Chloe, huh? Well, I'm sure there is some baggage somewhere then," I laughed.

"It wouldn't be so bad to have a cat," Steve added on a somewhat serious note.

Bethany and I both looked at him, but she beat me to the punch. "This may not work out between us," she deadpanned.

"Oh, for the love of God, they are not that bad. Don't forget, I've been shot." As he moved towards her to grab her hand, I thought: *Had he not been shot, I'm not sure she would have grabbed it.*

"I'm just hoping you are doped up on meds. Let's get back to the others," I said as I started my way to the table.

The skyline was forming a brilliant hue of colors momentarily masking the events of the day. The lighted décor of the patio provided a soft ambiance that made you want to sit for hours.

Daylight savings time had passed and fortunately the evening hours were extended a little longer on this spring evening. *If only we could stay.*

I surveyed everyone's face and emotions. It had been a long day already, and there would be no letup in the future.

"First, a moment of silence for our good friend, Doc." We bowed our heads in unison out of respect, while I silently prayed. I was the last to lift my head. When I did, all eyes were upon me. Determined.

"This should never have come to this. We signed up for this. Doc did not. Let's not forget the other three medical personnel that were on site and were unfortunate victims. Someone is either lazy, or they were sending a message after their failed attempt."

"My vote is on the latter," added a disheveled Steve.

"How astute. Killing me smalls. Try not to use both brain cells."

I met Jake and Steve in their early years of Navy Seal training out in California. Man, it feels like ages ago. Technically, I guess it has been ages. They both got me out of a few hairy-scary situations and would lay down their lives for me. We can quote movie and song lyrics with the best of them. When they left the service, they came to work for me and implemented an enhanced new "training program" that mimics what Bethany and I did eons ago. My children's training experience and overall well-being are in their direct care. I have the utmost respect for them. Both are physically good-looking beasts, and I can see why Bethany went for Steve, as he is the more comical one of the two. I wanted to slap him, at times, but he's like a kid brother. What can I say? After Jake got divorced, he became a little more introverted under that tough exterior, so I always had a softer spot for him. The mental things we each have endured and lost in protecting American's freedoms can be taxing. The statistics are alarming for veterans, with suicide rates at one and half times higher than non-veterans. He was tough, but I always had my eye out on him.

"We have a short window to make some progress. Let's talk about generalities, so everyone is on the same page before we get into specifics. Steve, I already discussed with Tom that you and he are meeting up with Ainsworth and Larkin to get the kids and find out more from our seven scientists. Tom will transfer the kids and dogs again, with Ainsworth's assist. Larkin can assist you in facilitating in getting answers from our mysterious seven."

"This should be fun. Have you heard that accent on Larkin? I can't understand him half the time. Are you sure he is even American?"

"His parents come from Irish decent, and I think they call it a "craic," versus "good time." It's Ainsworth you must worry about. He's not stable on a good day, and he will have been road tripping with the kids for days. That's more than enough for any sane person, which we know he isn't." We all laughed in acknowledgment, before I added, "Use whatever methods necessary to obtain who, where, and what we need from those scientists."

"On it," Steve responded.

"Bethany and I are taking the plane to redistribute the vials. The location will not be disclosed to anyone else for your own safety. Doc had sent over some of the testing results just prior, so Tom will work on deciphering that information while he and Ainsworth have the kids on the run."

Freddy had been quiet for a while. He had been my commander for decades, sending me on missions while concealing my identity, so now to be in a position where I told him what to do was quite the challenge. Not to mention that it was his love interest in my mother that brought all of this to fruition. My mother had been trained and worked for the US Treasury when she got brainwashed to enlist in a top-secret mission for the good of the American people. The lab experiment gone awry produced three children that were then separated and taken to different the corners of the world. Was it for New World Order, a new biological weapon, or the latest conspiracy in light of the pandemic; an alternative therapy suppression that involves the FDA suppressing natural cures due to the influence from the pharmaceutical industry? Bottom line: it didn't really matter. They all amount to…GREED. Freddy shielded me from all of this for decades, while silently wishing he was my biological father.

Freddy looked to me and asked, "Where do you want me?"

"It depends on if you can answer me this. Pull out your phone. Do you have a contact for this number? I asked as I showed him the 202 number from our deceased sniper."

"That's Intrator's private number." *Dammit, Go figure. I knew I recognized that number.*

Bethany looked at me, concerned, "It's the VP's private number, you sure?' she directed to Freddy.

Freddy already understood the implications as he nodded.

"It looks like you are going to DC to figure out what his involvement is with our KIA. Bethany and I will drop you off on our way out. We'll need to verify Borrelli's involvement, as well."

"You think the President is involved?" Freddy asked, earnest but skeptical.

"No, I don't, but I don't get paid to assume, and our lives are at stake, so he doesn't get a skip or pass until confirmation. We've done countless clandestine missions for him, and I trust him. He knows we have more information to bury him in a shitshow, if push came to shove."

Freddy was the master manipulator, and his vast contacts and reach were renowned. His loyalty was always to the "Administration," but I realized that he, too, had been manipulated over his decades of service.

Steve lightened the mood with his next statement. "Don't forget I need my stitches out, so you can hookup - I mean, visit nurse Erika."

"Sweet Jesus. Freddy, just make sure to wrap it up," Bethany piped up.

Freddy rolled his eyes as he shook his head, but he had a small grin on his face when he responded with, "Why, God, why?"

Jake looked at me solemnly and asked, "What about me?"

"You need to get your comatose girlfriend awake and to ante up. You'll be coordinating with Bes and Lily."

"What, specifically?"

"You have the most pressing task, right now. You need to track down my long-lost brothers. It's time we all met."

# SIX

WE STAYED AT NOLA'S FOR ANOTHER HOUR, fine tuning details and relishing the last moments before we headed our separate ways. Tom and I stole away to the bar to talk alone and to coordinate plans for our family. We had the custom of drinking a bottle of Abacus before each mission that we would be forgoing, as this wasn't that kind of establishment. They did have mystery shot night, so we opted to partake in that. Probably going to regret that decision; who knows what swill was in those bottles.

We called the kids to check in on their status. Matthew was first to answer with a hello in Mandarin. You could hear in the background that Mark was trying to grab his phone while Mary was yelling, "Mom, Dad, help me! I can't take them anymore."

I looked at Tom and shrugged, then silently laughed. All three complained about Ainsworth and his dog stinking up the car on the drive, and why did they have to leave in such a hurry. I gently reminded them that they'd fare worse out in the field, and to suck it up, buttercups. Just hearing their voices made me calmer and at peace. The three of them were excited that the labs would be joining them, too. They were probably more excited about that then seeing us. Had to remember not to take it personally. We caught up with them for a hot sec and told them Dad would rendezvous with them shortly, before hanging up with our standard, "Lo."

Tom looked at me holding my hands. We both dreaded this moment, knowing we had no control of upcoming events. Tom's looks resemble a cross between Henry Cavill and John Stamos. So, yeah: super funking hot. My looks had changed so many times over the years, it was hard to keep track. When we met, I was undercover on a mission and had brown contacts that he told me he was attracted by. To this day, I swear he thinks my eyes are green, even though they are distinctively blue. *Whatever.* Doc and other medical teams had rebuilt me so many times over the years from missions gone wrong. I had sick fucks take out teeth (a few times), I had a broken jaw, broken ribs, head lacerations, they'd pulled off toenails, broken my femur...to name a few things off the top of my head. I've had so many hair styles and colors changes; I could be a poster child for Loreal. Pretty damn good looking one, too, thanks to medical miracles.

But don't kid yourself. Money can do a lot, and the American government had invested a pretty penny in me. Currently, I was rocking a chestnut mid-back-length hair style and was certainly in the best physical shape I've been in decades. Being genetically created, after this virus hit, it was clear that I was mutating. My wounds and scars were disappearing, if not all together gone. My speed and strength were increasing with age versus declining. Hell, even the dead comedian, George Carlin, stated, over thirty years ago that viruses only mutate after vaccines. *No shit. I'm living proof.* I had a Jennifer Lawrence look going on from *Red Sparrow*. I could live with that. Tom seemed to highly approve, too. Just saying.

"I don't like when we have to split up, but I know it's necessary," Tom whispered in my ear as he held me in a tight embrace.

Trying to lighten the mood, I responded with, "Don't worry, the kids will be with you to protect you."

It elicited the response I was hoping for as he pulled back laughing, knuckling me in the ribs. "Dammit Matti, I'm trying to be serious for a moment."

"I know, love," I started solemnly. "Hopefully, it will go quick if all goes as planned. We got this. Everybody counts or no one counts."

"Did you just quote *Bosch*? You really need help." He laughed as he pulled me back closer and kissed me.

The last time we'd said something like this, I was gone for one year. It weighed on us very deeply. Not just us, but our whole family and all those surrounded by us. It fueled my "passion." Know what the difference is between vengeance and revenge? Nothing, really: one is considered a noun versus the other is a verb. It's inflicting punishment for being wronged. It was time to use the verb form.

"One last mystery shot for good measure?" he asked.

"Oh, hell no. They are called mystery shots for a reason, as I have no idea what the 'f was in that in that last one."

We got up to join the gang in the back. The owner had already picked up our tab. *We love this place.* As we walked out to the vehicles, we noticed a few neighborhood friendlies dawdling the back alleys. We'd started parting to each respective vehicle, when an overtly anxious one came towards Freddy and grabbed his arm while wielding a knife. Jake, Steve, Bethany, and I already had our guns sighted on this forehead before he was able to lift up his knife.

As I moved a red laser beam from his head to his manhood, I inquired, "You want it in your head, or a free sex change?"

Like rats, his other friends skittered off in the night as our would-be attacker cowered, and he backed slowly away before running frantically in the opposite direction.

"Thought you were going to go with 'I see dead people.'" Jake said, laughing.

"That one works, too. Welp, that's one way to start our journey. Steve, send us out on a good one," I requested.

"Oh, I got this…," he said as he jumped into the driver's seat and paired his phone, which blared over his speakers.

*Rage Against the Machine, Killing in the Name…Some of those that work forces, are the same that burn crosses, Killing in the Name of, Killing in the Name of…*

Freddy looked at me as he mouthed, "Psyche eval, pronto."

I looked to Bethany and mouthed, "That's your man."

# SEVEN

BETHANY, FREDDY, AND I parted for the private terminal to board the Gulfstream. Our first destination was to drop off Freddy in DC. We were traveling with Koda and Bruiser, too, as we needed their assistance in part two of our travels.

While Bethany navigated, it allowed ample time for Freddy and me to discuss theories and strategies. Amongst other things.

The current scene in the airplane was strangely reminiscent when I first met Freddy in person. We had just left Darvos, Switzerland for a private meeting that consisted of the Director of the NSA, Deputy Director of CIA, and a bevy of Presidents and who's who from every country; no shocker here...except China.

In the meeting, the Russian counterpart to our NSA just had his head split in two. As a result, it was how I learned "my creation" was a greed so grand in nature, it's hard for any human to process. Collective beings/countries gathered to forge an alliance to demonstrate that science would obliterate religion. Don't worry, I eventually tracked down and took care of the Director of the NSA and Deputy Director of CIA who had coming what they justly deserved. *How's that for science?*

It was on the plane ride home that I first encountered this man, Freddy, who had orchestrated everything in my life up to that point. Freddy was involved in the genesis of all this madness. He was the background player in my early years as I lived with my aunt and uncle, and arranged specialized training when it was confirmed that I was indeed "special." Similar to Clark Kent finding out he had skills in *Superman*, it became evident early on that I was hitting on higher mental and physical levels than my peers. *Then again, I was being brought up in Mississippi...* Freddy became my commander after he sent me into instruction at the Academy. *Thank God I met Bethany there.* At one point, I even thought he was my biological father, only to find out he was just a hopeless romantic in love with my mother fielding her dying request to look after me. Could have been a scene straight from *Harry Potter*, with Snape.

My mother, in a moment of clarity, realized that this genetic creation of human bodies would never bode well. How apropos that the original experiment was orchestrated for twin boys resulting in triplets, with the female holding the dominate gene. Although my mother could not destroy the children she bore, she ensured that they would be separated so no one (or country) could ever reproduce again, then proceeded to detonate a Sarin nerve gas bomb, killing herself and all the personnel involved in the invention. (VX nerve agent was developed specifically for military use, but was not manufactured and deployed until later. The US "allegedly" doesn't use it, but ask any SEAL team member...)

So, here I sat with Freddy, again discerning lies and truths, but needing and wanting to trust this man that has been in my life since conception – literally and figuratively. His mission was to determine what role Vice President Intrator had in the hit (and or otherwise), and if President Borrelli had any affiliation with it. From news conferences, you could tell that Intrator could talk your ear off, but I personally couldn't see his involvement on any level. Between Borrelli and Intrator, they were covered up, trying to recover from their assassination attempt and subsequent suicide of Pres-elect. It was a shit show, plain and simple.

"You have any working theories?" he asked as he handed over to me a Glenfeddich 18 on the rocks. *Just like last time.*

"Let's start with you. What do you think?" I rebuked.

He started, "I think it's telling that they sent a women sniper."

"I do, too, but maybe for different reasons. What are yours?"

"There are probably around three hundred known men snipers. As for women…well, my guess would be maybe eight or nine tops that are qualified but that certainly doesn't mean 'active.' She was no Chris Kyle. You're the only 'woman' I know that could pull it off," he said, using air quotes.

"I'm not sure air quotes were needed for 'woman', but I get your point,' I chided. "I've never asked Jake and Steve what they thought about him. My bad. Of course, his kills were militarily recorded. Mine, not so much. Just saying. But…I agree. Looks like we were both thinking along the same lines. We'll know more after Tom is able to drill down, but let's play out some scenarios. Even though she had Russian gear, she didn't look it…well, from the bits that were identifiable. If so, that doesn't bode well for us."

"Yes, Bethany could have used a little more constraint – not that it will matter," he offered.

"So, American gone rogue, possibly? Disgruntled? Family ties to any one of the mother f'ers we've taken out? Or is it someone foreign with the same questions, but different motivations?" I offered.

"What did her teeth look like?" he inquired.

I had to smirk and got up and opened the door to the cockpit. "Hey B, can you recall what our sniper's teeth looked like?"

"Goddammit. You told me to shoot, I shot. No one said to protect the damn teeth. Shut the door, you're officially on my last nerves. Spent a year protecting YOUR family and NOW need to fly this damn plane. Never mind, I'll do it myself," she growled as she slammed the door shut.

With my hands in the air at mid-section, I said to Freddy, "That would be a negative, ghost rider. Not able to determine. Talk to me, Dad," I said as I put my hand to my head in despair.

He shook his head and laughed, "All of you are seriously need of help. Was that a *Top Gun* reference, or the new *Maverick*?"

"Does it matter?" I deadpanned. With raised eyebrows, I added, "Moving on: when you get to DC, I've arranged for you to meet up with Sedlin and Long to gather some more intel before proceeding."

"You sure about them two?"

Sedlin and Long were long-term military officers now serving as Director and Deputy Director of Operations for in the CIA. They'd both previously worked under the traitor Tammy Carter, who was a previous Deputy Director. She was a different breed, alright. Freddy hooked up with her one time supposedly for 'mission intel' *(yeah...that one needs air quotes...)*. She had a twin fetish, and orchestrated, with other nations this CRISPR, biological weapon, religious overturning, or whatever this ongoing damn conspiracy was that we had going on. (Come to think of it, we took her out in a Tom Cruise, *Mission Impossible II*, manner when we disguised her as Freddy. Is it art imitating reality, or the other way around? *Just saying.*)

"You're the one that made the initial introductions to them. Hell, I trust them as much as I trust you at this point," I expressed incredulously.

"Touché. I'll take that in the positive light I'm sure you meant," he winked.

"We all have choices to make," I winked back.

# EIGHT

ONCE WE DROPPED OFF FREDDY, we refueled, got provisions, and let the dogs run for a bit. Bethany had to submit a flight plan, and looked at me for direction.

"Ok, where are we heading?"

"You're probably not going to like this…" I stalled.

"No shit."

"We're heading back to Jerusalem."

"Mother…," she said as she shook her head. "We're going back to where we first hid the vials? Why didn't we just leave them there?"

"As with most things in life, we made choices and decisions based on the information we had at hand at the time. We're not returning them to the same location, but we are going to return to that city for their protection. I need to confirm an additional stop on the way."

"Why? FAB can make the whole jaunt."

"FAB? What?"

"That's what I named her: FAB. Fast Ass Bitch. She can handle the whole trip."

"FAB? Holy shit. That's why we don't let you come up with call signs. That's the best you got?"

"Hey, now," she meekly protested, as she knew I was right.

FAB (aka the Gulfstream) has a range of seventy-five hundred nautical miles or fourteen hours. The distance from DC to Jerusalem was fifty-two hundred miles and just over twelve hours. If only the US could get with the rest of the world in their other damn conversion tables. A nautical mile is slightly longer than a mile on land. *Why do we always over-complicate things?*

"Submit flight plan for Naples, Whop-eye."

"I've told you repeatedly that we need another call sign for me, or you can fly this damn plane yourself," she protested with a laugh as she fiddled with the instrument panel. *Her one eye was a little off...She really did love me.*

"As I just mentioned, we made choices and decisions based on the information we had at hand."

"You really are on my last nerve. Leaving in ten, wench."

"Love you, too."

The cockpit of G650 is not as sexy as you might envision. I mean, it's not luxury-luxury in this part of the plane, even though it does have some sweet bells and whistles. For this flight, it required one pilot to fly and the other to read charts and communicate with air traffic control. Bethany and Tom purchased this while I was MIA. Hell, the annual costs to operate were a fortune, at two hundred flying hours per year. We were beating those hours easily. Fuel costs alone were fifty percent of the costs and were now considerably higher in the recent gas market debacle. *WTF.* Bethany was already hinting of wanting to trade up to obtain the G700. *Fat chance.*

I situated Koda and Bruiser on the leather sofas that faced each other. They would have preferred to stay up in the cockpit with us, but there just wasn't ample room. I checked in with Tom to determine his status with the kids. He was just a few hours out from them. I would feel better when they were all together. I called the kids to check on them, as was customary before any flight departure, now. *You leave your kids for a year; you change your habits.* Just hearing their voices, gave me peace. Despite them arguing about why they had to relocate again.

I joined Bethany up front and settled in for the ride. The sky is always brilliant from up here, be it day or night, but I prefer nights. The lights from the city, in conjunction with the horizon and stars, were breathtaking every time. Transports you to another time or place.

Bethany felt the same way too. I think that's why she loved flying. It was her happy place, her peace, her heaven. We both just stared out in the distance and sat in hushed awe before she broke the silence.

"We're going to Jerusalem because of the eagle, aren't we?" she silently inquired.

After all these years, there was no one that knew me better. As much as we kidded each other, we could still finish each other's thoughts.

"Yes."

"Walk me through your thought process," she requested without judgment.

"Remember that old joke…the one where there was a flood, and the homeowner dies as he was waiting for a sign? And God said, I sent you a life vest, a boat, and helicopter…"

"Yeah, person was an idiot. Natural selection, if you ask me. Here's your sign," she joked.

"Seriously, B. How sad it is that I taught my kids at an early age to check your six? That's messed up. It's now mass shootings, gun control, sexual orientation, riots…bottom line, though, it's our culture. It's centered on greed and evil. I feel like we have signs all over us lately, but just haven't noticed. For example, we have seven scientists. We have seven countries. We have an eagle flying over us…" I trailed off.

"If I'm following your logic, seven is the sign of hundred percent in the Bible, right? Tribulation is seven years. Are you seriously thinking that we are about to experience the rapture? Because if so, hallelujah; there's no need to worry about recycling anymore, and who cares where we dump these vials?"

I had to laugh. It did sound crazy. "I'm not saying we are there… just that, technically, we have reached all the milestones needed to be there…" I trailed off. "I just feel like we haven't been paying attention to ALL the signs. This triplet thing has me obsessing, too."

"In tribulation, if memory serves correct, doesn't it repeat of a third? Third of the rivers, third of water, third of land. Light not shined for a third of the time. Three trumpets to signal…yadda, yadda," she added.

"Yep, an eagle announces the last three trumpets, too," I added.

"Wait, don't go cherry picking. You're smarter than that. I know that finding out you had two brothers has messed you up, but you're not that special. Plus, don't forget, we'd better not be here if there is a rapture, and you won't need to worry about the ol' U-S-A as I'm confident it'll be wiped out in the first third. Wait, you just finished studying Revelations, didn't you?" she asked as she shrugged her shoulders.

We are all victims of what we read or are shown. One can't respond with wisdom until you know what is truly going on and know it is unfiltered of bias. I once read that, in the world of propaganda, the truth is always a conspiracy. My whole life was one big conspiracy after another.

"I'm sure I'm just tired and over-thinking some things. Fell asleep the other day watching, *Bruce Almighty*. Probably taking the line of...*Want a miracle? Be the miracle*...to heart too much."

"Don't placate me with that 'tired shit'," she demanded. "I know you better. You just don't want to discuss it now. I know what you are thinking. The G7 summit, aren't you? Another damn seven."

"Close, but actually...I'm thinking a little farther down the line with the prophecy of ten kings. An eleventh comes and kicks out three. The Antichrist and seven countries remain."

"Jesus Christ, and you think Steve need's help," she responded

"Hey, now."

"Oh stop. HE knows I'm a believer. I just cuss and drink a little. Let's break for a hot sec. Turn on some music."

We both stared out at the night sky as Kansas's *Dust in the Wind* came on... *Now, don't hang on, Nothing lasts forever but the earth and sky. It slips away, all your money won't another minute buy*...

Bethany turned to me. "I know, damn signs."

I simply responded with, "Just saying..."

# NINE

WE LANDED IN NAPLES to meet with Bes and Lily and confer with them prior to departing for Jerusalem. Bethany stayed back to handle the plane, while I caught up with them inside the private terminal.

Bessum was the head of the Albanian mafia, and his cousin, Lily, was now the head of the Sicilian mafia due to her husband's lifetime incarceration. Her husband still ran things, but don't kid yourself: my intel had her putting him in prison in the first place.

Bes and Lily weren't my blood, but they felt like blood to me over the years as we worked on various missions that supported both our causes. I feared the day when we didn't have a mutual cause. Afterall, blood is blood, and we were not.

Once Tom had more genetic make-up details from the lab testing, it would assist Bess, Lily and Jake in locating my brothers. At birth, one brother was taken to Russia while the other brother was handed off to the CIA, who they then delivered to Mexico. They were both highly trained operatives as well.

Bes, in his usual direct fashion, started the conversation in his distinct dialect. "I assume you want me to track down brother of Mother Russia."

Lily was quick to add, "We're going to have a problem if you even think I'm going to Mexico."

Julius Caesar was the infamous one who is attributed to the "divide and conquer" phrase, a line as old as politics and war.

Of course, Sun Tzu stated in the "The Art of War" that your impact is weakened as you are divided and conquered.

"I don't want you divide on this op. You'll need to work collectively starting in Russia to track down sibling number 2. His current name has changed multiple times. He was previously going by Jardani, but now appears to be using 'Renat.' We also need to know how many children he has fathered, if any. Jake will focus on Mexico, David, or sibling number three," I started.

"You American's have too many code signs with Alpha, Bravo, Omega, etc. Which name we tracking? I don't want to be confused with number two." Bes added.

"I can see why that would confuse you," his cousin smirked.

*God, grant me serenity.*

"Renat is a good Russian name," Bes dismissed, and continued.

I've always been fascinated by name origins. Some names really did seem to be applicable to their humans. It's like when you select a dog, and the dog resembles its owner. Coincidence, or cosmic? Renat, in Russian translates to 'a reborn man'.

*Damn signs.*

"Fine, Renat it is…for now. Let's just hope he doesn't choose to go by Avraam."

"Why, what does that mean?" Lily inquired.

"Father of many."

"We getting paid our expected customary fee? If so, he can have a hundred kids as far as we're concerned," she indicated.

*Greed. It always comes down to money.*

"Let's hope he's sterile. You'll get paid when you identify and locate…Bonus with a successful exfil. Extra kicker if you manage to do it quickly, including any possible offspring."

Lily got up, "No sense wasting time. We have what we need to get started, and will confer with Tom on results."

My eyes did a double take when she stood up. Something was noticeably different.

"How many weeks?"

Lily was visibly taken aback by my question, but answered coolly and promptly. "Twelve."

*Ahh shit.* I doubted there were conjugal visits in the prison where her husband was being held. Blood is blood and this one wouldn't be. Did she need the additional money to cut and run, or how was she going to handle it? *Oh, good Lord, was it from one of the Chinese diplomats she suffocated during her kinky role play?*

Taking bets that hubby was going to meet up with an unfortunate accident. Some things were better left unknown and unsaid.

"Congratulations. You're right, best be getting to it." I stood up and walked the hell out.

# TEN

BACK ON FAB, Bethany had everything prepped and ready to go. Koda and Bruiser were back in their spots, and we departed promptly for Jerusalem. We had just under six more hours until arrival.

Tom had successfully retrieved the kids and was with Ainsworth in the process of setting up our TOC (Tactical Operations Center). We needed eyes everywhere, operating in five different time zones. The kids would be obtaining first-hand experience and knowledge that was not normally privy to them at this stage in their training. In the past, Freddy had always coordinated with an unspecified crew. New leadership, what can I say?

Bethany and I were rehashing our training in comparison to the kids. By the end of fourth year, the kids would go through a similar SERE training that we endured. Survival, Evasion, Resistance, and Escape (SERE) training is used to return with honor in survival scenarios. As Tier One Ops, Jake and Steve went through the same training as SEALS. I never discussed this with Tom.

It all started innocently. We were nearing completion of our training program in Minot, North Dakota. We trained separately and outside of but in conjunction with the Air Force Global Strike Command located at Minot AFB. Bethany and I had been out celebrating as we were informed of our first assignment. Weather was perfect. All was right in the world. We tied one on pretty good. *I still can't drink Jägermeister to this day, but boy, she can.*

We were stumbling back to our quarters when we were abducted. Six men took turns beating the shit out of us, wanting what information we had on about Alexander Klauser, who was our primary target for our first mission. He was a human sex trafficker and a seller of arms.

Neither Bethany nor I had received any intel at that point: just that our deployment would be to Zurich. It didn't matter. They continued to take turns beating and berating us. They wanted info on our training, the base, the commanders, the set-up. We provided nothing. This went on for hours, on and off. You lose concept of time. You just want the pain to stop. You can't think anymore, much less worry about this return with honor shit.

I can still viscerally recall the pain; physically, mentally, and emotionally.

When nothing was divulged, that's when the interrogation was stepped up. Bethany and I were crammed into black oil drums filled with water. Stripped down to just our underwear, we were stuffed into these drums. The lids were secured on by scorching blow torches. Gasping for air for hours, trying to hold your head up, while not passing out. Bethany and I would occasionally try to shout out and encourage each other, but the music was too loud and they would hammer on the top when they heard us, further increasing the pain to our ear drums and our beaten psyches.

We were then loaded onto a cargo plane and travelled for hours to an unknown destination, which we were led to believe was Zurich. Heavy metal rock music blared constantly. We were gasping and counting the seconds.

Being confined is one thing, being sleep deprived another. Now, add in the physical pain. But just wait, there's more. They don't prep you by saying, "this is only a drill." The emotional element is the kicker.

When we landed, they pried my lid off and told me they would shoot Bethany if I didn't supply them with the information they were wanting. You have only milli seconds, under the worst possible combination of conditions to consider your actions and consequences. I offered nothing and they repeatedly shot the drum next to me until all the water spilled out and I heard the wailing stop.

A tear rolled down my already soaked face. I premonition that I was the reason Don McLean wrote *American Pie…Them good old boys were drinking whiskey and rye, Singing, "This'll be the day that I die"…This will be the day that I die…*

I had nothing left; they could take me now; I was ready. They would get nothing from me.

Another barrel was rolled in, and they barked that they would shoot this innocent bystander next. The hairs on the back of my neck were standing up again. I was sworn to serve and protect, but you can't reason with crazy. My mouth was so swollen and my arms like jelly, when I whispered for them to come closer, and I'd tell them what they needed.

I can still recall his face. Looming over at six two, full beard, brown eyes, bulking muscles, he smiled that crooked, winning smile as he approached me. My eyes swollen shut, my mouth worse off, I whispered again that I would tell him. His smile broadened as he turned around to tell the others, "I told you I'd crack her." Before he could turn back to me, I already had my bra off and wrapped around his neck twice to suffocate this sick son of a bitch, while using every living ounce I had to grab his San Viper pistol. His arms struggled while he tried to defend the choke hold while flailing to retrieve his pistol that I now held to his temple. The barrel started to topple over, the others realizing that the weight of the barrel with my weight would snap his thick neck. That's when Master Gunnery Sergeant Wilson came running out and shouted "Matti, STOP!!! This is a drill."

Was it a mirage? Was it real? I let go. Lucky for him.

They all clapped and saluted as they helped me out and brought Bethany in, who had successfully endured the same treatment with similar results. The emotions were overwhelming. Each of the others understood as they themselves had been through this. You come out different, but I can't say better. It changes you.

We hadn't talked about this in years - hell, decades. Bethany looked over to me. "The shit we've done, right? Couldn't forget Klauser after all that, even if we wanted to. Psycho was going to throw me off the building."

"If I recall correctly, he was going to rag tag you first and you pretended to jump before I used my MK and put a permanent mark on his head."

"You seriously need help. I can't believe you can recall what rifle you used."

"You're my best friend, so maybe we should ask for a group discount." I laughed.

The time reminiscing had made the flight quick. We landed an hour early and were checking flight records when she offered up, "Since we made up some time getting here, before we head out, I could use a drink. What do you think?"

Tom was pinging us on the secure line, so I told her, "I'm game. Hold that thought."

"Hey, love, how's it going?"

The line was crystal clear, but no voice was coming over. "Tom, you there?"

I could feel his fear and hesitation. The dogs alertly came barreling to the cockpit doors. They sensed something wrong too. *If only humans could be as well trained in human emotion.*

"Oh God. Matti. I don't know how to tell you this." His voice was struggling.

"Tom, what happened?! Please."

"Matti…it's your parents…"

"What happened!"

"Matti," he stammered as he tried to continue, "reports are just coming in saying they were killed in an automobile crash. Eyewitnesses said they were run off the road purposefully and the driver took off. Car exploded immediately on impact. I'm trying to pull up video now. Matti, by all preliminary accounts, they were targeted. This was a hit."

"Tom, listen to me carefully. Make sure no one followed you or Ainsworth with the kids. Double and triple check. Ensure all safety measures. Tell Ainsworth to prep for Armageddon. I need to check on something and will call you right back. I love you," I said, and hung up.

SERE training teaches you many things. Not to panic is one, but I'd just entered my own DEFCON II.

# ELEVEN

BETHANY WAS ALREADY PULLING UP SATELLITE while I tried to get ahold of Tia. Tia, or Tresa Peterson, came to protect and assist me at an early age, for training purposes. I'm talking at the age of eight here. Like I've said, the government has invested significantly in me in all stages of my life. We called her Tia ('aunt' in Spanish), as she moved from Mississippi from Alabama and had to have some reason why she lived with us, so honorary 'aunt' she became. No one questioned in Mississippi that fact that she was person of color, and we were not.

Although Tia wasn't officially on around the clock protection for my parents, she was stipend heavily to this day and more importantly, she enjoyed being with my parents as they were closer in age. She had recently started a long-distance relationship with Aldo, who was the former head of the High Camorra. He was a longtime associate and friend to me with some benefits to us all.

No answer. *Shit.*

"B, pull up video. I want a full SSE in motion. See who we can contact on the ground if we need to."

"Already on it, wait five secs. I'm also getting audio recording from the live feed from the attending officer."

We watched thermal imaging video from a highway camera and compared to the live feed. The car was definitely my parents' white

Ford 150 truck. They were on vacation, and this appeared to be driving on Highway 129 in Charlotte, North Carolina. The highway is known as "The Dragon" for the three hundred and eighteen curves in an eleven-mile stretch. Thousands visit each year for the beauty of the Smoky Mountains despite how treacherous it is.

We could make out two people in front, but they were not recognizable. We then saw a black, Cadillac Escalade with black-out windows cut off several vehicles as it approached near the truck at express speed and swerved to the inside lane. They knew exactly when to hit to steer the truck off the mountain. This was no accident. We watched as the truck quickly was engulfed in flames before it exploded. Bethany grabbed my arm as a natural reaction.

I sat staring at the video, before I barked, "Something is off. My parents wouldn't be driving at night. Get the body cam and audio up from the officer."

A quick couple more keystrokes and we were linked to the audio and body cam recording. Sounded like a junior officer was at the scene first. He was in shock, staring at the charred remains. He was describing his initial thoughts how this may have occurred as he circled the vehicle, marking off a perimeter.

"B, go back to where he was on driver side door. Zoom in to the ground. What is that?"

"It looks like crushed beer cans. Maybe whiskey bottles?"

*Breathe in, breathe out.* There is no conceivable way for the bodies to be as charred as they were without an additional accelerant. Not enough time from the explosion, which impacted more of the bed of the truck. My parents didn't drink. They didn't drive at night. Whoever did this wanted it to look like a drunk driving accident. They would pay.

Just then, my phone rang. Tia was returning my call. "Matti, no worries, child. I have your parents."

"What? How?" I asked as relief flooded over me.

"They called to tell me their truck had been stolen. I fetched them up immediately and took them to a secure location. This accident happened shortly thereafter. It appears that whoever it was, wanted a reaction out of you before you could confirm. Probably was hoping you'd still be in the air and unable to verify remotely, being nighttime here. I didn't tell your parents about the incident. I didn't want to shake them up."

"Tia, you're a lifesaver. Literally. Thank you. I'll need you to extend your vacation with them a bit longer while we sort some things out. Maybe you could take them to go visit Aldo?" ...*and his armed mafia posse.*

"One step ahead of you. Already decided and told them we were changing up our vacation schedule. I thought they'd want to check out Ft. Bragg."

*Headquarters of Delta Force.* "But of course, you're the best. Tell our friends, hello."

"Will do, and true," she lightheartedly replied.

# TWELVE

TOM PROBABLY GAINED TEN YEARS back to his life when I called him and gave him the news. Having lost his parents and siblings in a plane crash, no one wants to give or receive these types of calls.

Tom and Ainsworth had everything set up and were now digging in deeper to our KIA and lab results from Doc's office. We really needed for them to uncover a marker or anything to help narrow down the field in the search for my brothers. The kids developed a new liking to Ainsworth during their road trip comparing him to Sonny in *Seal Team*. They thought his dog had IBS.

Bethany reached out to Steve and he and Larkin were on task with the scientists. It was a fine line knowing when to push and when you had exceeded their physical and mental boundaries. Both were quick to point out the infamous Spock phrase from *The Wrath of Khan...Logic clearly dictates that the needs of the many outweigh the needs of the few...* There was no doubt that either would pull a trigger if it was deemed necessary.

Bethany and I adorned our new wardrobe consisting of long flowing dresses, sandals and head-covering. Koda and Bruiser fit right in, as a third of Israel were dog owners. *Well, if you consider a Shih Tzu or Pekinese dogs.*

We would be traveling by foot to the Cenacle of Mount Zion. Many westerners don't know it by this name – rather, the site of the

Last Supper of Jesus and the coming of the Holy Spirit to the apostles (first church). The Cenacle is on the upper floor of a two-story building above the Tomb of King David. Just as portrayed in the movie *The Da Vinci Code*, a conspiracy was kindled and derived from Leonardo Da Vinci's portrait of the Last Supper. *Granted, the movie is a work of fiction with some factual elements.* Although the original debate was over who was beside Jesus? Was it the apostle John or Mary Magdalene? What continued to be other source of speculations - were there other encoded secrets embedded in the portrait? *As a matter of fact, yes.*

The Cenacle is divided into six rib-vaulted bays with freestanding columns. A column shaft in the Cenacle's interior wall is completely independent of the wall, leading scholars, and engineers to consider the possibility that this wall was not original to the building.

Each apostle had a different reaction portrayed in the painting. Why was doubting Thomas pointing up, in the picture? Foreshadowing the resurrection, or something more simplistic? Hence, we were provided clues to where we would be depositing the airtight, fireproof, waterproof receptacle that no entity has been able to locate for decades. *There are signs everywhere.*

For sixty US dollars, you can get a half-day tour where it begins at the holy place of the Last Supper. While the tour proceeded, we left the group to complete our task at hand.

# THIRTEEN

TIME TO CHECK IN ON FREDDY...

Back on FAB, we contacted Freddy before we took off to see what progress he had made. He'd contacted Sedlin and Long and they were meeting up for drinks that evening. They were all close in age, so maybe he'd acquire some new friends from old associates.

Sedlin was scouring through records and reports on the VP and Pres. The Secret Service is responsible for guarding the President and Vice President (amongst others). They monitor all their movement. Unless they are violating a crime, Secret Service really won't do anything about it, even if the President is a drunk whoremonger. *Had a few of those.*

Established in 1865, the Secret Service was originally created as a Bureau of the Treasury Department to subdue counterfeiting. It wasn't until 1901 that they were tasked with protection for the President. In 2003, the Secret Service was transferred to the Department of Homeland of Security. Why now? Well, immediately after the attacks of 9/11, TSA was created (Transportation Security Administration). TSA collets all your personal information: where you are coming and going, birth dates, social security numbers, passport, airline, credit cards, children, and spouse information. So, you have two departments that are basically your government versions of Google and Alexa knowing everything about you.

Let's revisit the US Constitution that you must do twenty Google drop-down searches on to find the exact wording, since it is now buried…*Signs everywhere (Holy shit)…*

*"We the People of the United States, in Order to form a more perfect Union, establish Justice, insure domestic Tranquility, provide for the common defense, promote the general Welfare, and secure the Blessings of Liberty to ourselves and our Posterity, do ordain and establish this Constitution for the United States of America."*

The first three words are the emphasis, We the People. Doesn't say Government now, does it? The government's creation and main role was to protect these rights and, if not, 'We the People', have the right to revolt. The Constitution and Bill of Rights established a government. The Declaration of Independence was for breaking away from government when it was not serving the people.

Let's keep digging deeper with the Bill of Rights. How many can you say off the top of your head? Hint: There's ten. Can you name all ten? *Liar.* Sadly, most can only name the first two.

## ■ The Bill of Rights

| | |
|---|---|
| 1st: | Guarantees freedom of religion, speech, press, assembly, and petition |
| 2nd: | Guarantees right to bear arms |
| 3rd: | Prohibits quartering of troops in private homes |
| 4th: | Protects people from unreasonable searches and seizures |
| 5th: | Guarantees due process for accused persons |
| 6th: | Guarantees the right to a speedy and public trial in the state where the offense was committed |
| 7th: | Guarantees the right to jury trial for civil cases tried in federal courts |
| 8th: | Prohibits excessive bail and cruel and unusual punishments |
| 9th: | Provides that people have rights beyond those stated in the Constitution |
| 10th: | Provides that powers not granted to the national government belong to the states and to the people |

The US Government was created with the 'intent' to protect the American people, just like Facebook was created with the 'intent' to bring people together. What changed? *One guess...starts with G.*

If the VP was involved in our KIA, Freddy would have to assess if there had been another breech, and in which department. I personally had been involved in ops with CIA, NSA, and a few other "A's that had been infiltrated by foreign countries. To date, the Secret Service has never recorded a traitor. Key word: Recorded. The Secret Service has daily summary reports for the Pres and VP. Trick was there were over fifty agents they would need to scour records for, on upward of a year.

Since 1973, the VP's living residence is on the grounds of the United States Naval Observatory, so Freddy would have multiple locations to observe, and the clock was ticking.

*Don't kid yourself, he thrived under pressure.*

Back in the cockpit, Bethany quickly had us at thirty-five thousand feet, and put us on autopilot. I caught her up on Freddy's activities when we were abruptly alerted there was signal lock on us.

"Fuck! We're painted. Grab the pack and chutes and brace for impact!" Bethany exclaimed.

Bethany had installed super-expensive anti-missile measures on FAB. I had bitched about it when I originally heard the costs, since most private planes don't have and can't detect an incoming missile at supersonic speeds. Simple math: this plane went six hundred ten miles per hour at max speed; a surface-to-air missile can go five times faster than speed of sound, or one mile per second. *We're fucked.*

I commanded the dogs, grabbed the chutes, and placed masks on each of our respective faces before Bethany attempted to divert and do a nosedive to get us to an acceptable HAHO jump (High

Altitude, High Opening). Another useful tidbit of information; a private aircraft is not generally known for jumps.

We'd be jumping from the over-wing emergency exit and within seconds pulling chutes, hoping not to be scorched by the incoming missile.

*Defcon II. Don't Panic.*

# FOURTEEN

3.2.1. WE STEPPED OFF just moments before impact.

Koda and Bruiser are trained in HAHO jumps. It's amazing that these trained dogs don't feel or express fear as humans do. They adorned a Kevlar vest, load-bearing harness that attached securely to each of us, and specialized goggles and oxygen mask that secured to their faces.

The last time I jumped out of an airplane, I was also targeted, and one hundred and fifty innocent victims were gassed before we brought the plane down and I projected the terrorist into the engine to make him fish food. I was getting tired of this crap.

Most jumps are pre-calculated for altitude, speed, distance, terrain. We were doing this on the fly (literally), with only a GPS to guide us while we traversed up to forty miles, hoping (praying) to land in ally-friendly territory. Now factor in wind. Currently, we were tracking to land on land versus in the Mediterranean Sea.

Bethany had sent an SOS to the team from the plane before we jumped, so they would be aware of our situation and would be making plans for successful exfil. Poor Tom, over the years and the number of times he had to worry before receiving any information or confirmation.

We were now crossing with no comms available, and were using hand signals to each other to guide our descent. With the weight of our gear and the dogs, we had roughly one hundred and ten extra pounds to navigate. It's a simple thing called 'gravity' at a certain point. Mental note: the kids had to stop giving Koda and

Bruiser extra snacks. They felt like they'd put on an extra five pounds, and didn't need to get in competition with our overweight labs.

Bethany and I sighted a large park and were trying to steer and stick a landing. Turns out, it was Hayarkon Park in Tel Aviv. Another two and half miles and we would have landed in the sea. As a heavily visited park, despite the early morning hour, we surprised a few people as we touched down. They were undecided between being curious or fearful, as we both had MP7's sticking out of our packs. They scurried, we scurried, we all scurried. We quickly ditched the chutes, threw a head covering on and went looking for an area to recoup and make contact as sunrise was coming.

Freddy had assets on the ground that fetched us to trek back to Ben Gurion Airport which was a thirty-minute commute. We arranged an Airbus A400M transport for the first leg back en route to DC. Not our normal accommodations. The Airbus is a four-engine turboprop.

Both wiped from the events, B looked to me with a disapproving nod to indicate she wasn't thrilled with the accommodations. "Glad I added that anti-missile detection now, aren't you? Too soon to talk about the G7?" she asked with a squeamish smile.

"Yeah, too soon." *It was going to be a long haul back.*

# FIFTEEN

"YOU PINPOINT, YET, who tried to blow us out of the fucking sky?" I asked Jake, feeling tired and exasperated.

"Working out the details. We obtained video footage from your detour in Naples. Service crew member who was refueling is seen placing what appears to be a tracker on your plane. Went farther back and it appears they followed Lily into the terminal."

"Who's following up?"

"It wasn't really an option. Lily was returning at her demand."

I immediately had visual of a deranged pregnant woman going in. If anyone thought she was unstable before, God help them now. If nothing else, I was confident she would get what was needed.

"Sweet Jesus. Ok, status update on tracking down Brother 2."

"You'll be happy, we've made some progress. We scrutinized video footage of the mom's nursing home. Chanlor was huge help, and was the one who noticed based on his walk. Seems like her dad, your brother David, has been pulling a Julia Roberts."

"Hmm. Master of disguises just like in *Sleeping with the Enemy*. Makes sense. I told you that he'd be fiercely loyal."

"We're following up on leads from the two times we've identified him. Six months apart. If he keeps up with this schedule, we may have another actual sighting coming up on the premises."

"Great work, Jake. Be careful. He's trained, just like us. And others are looking for him, too. If he's keeping eyes on the wife, you can be certain he's looking for his daughter. Keep Chanlor on watch. Don't be collateral damage."

"Matti, there's more," he trailed off.

"Spill it. This day can't get any worse. Just don't tell me he looks like Patrick Bergin. The guy gave me the creeps in that movie."

"Chanlor confessed something else. Your brother has another daughter. She fled the same time as whoever beat the shit tar out of the mother, and has been off radar ever since."

"Dammit, Jake. I told you your relationship with Chanlor would cloud your judgment. How did we miss that little nugget? Press her: she knows where her sister is; she's been playing you."

"I don't think she is, Matti. I get the impression that this brother of yours came to the same conclusion you did. By all accounts, he's acted to eliminate threats for freedom while trying to keep his family intact. You've been more successful on that front. I think he has the other daughter in hiding with him."

"Verdict is still out right now. I'm only focused on my family."

"You're the only family I have Matti. If I even get a whiff that something is off, I'll gladly pull the trigger on her myself. With no hesitation."

Sleeping with the Enemy's chilling theme song, *Berlioz - Symphonie fantastique 5th Movement* played in my head...no words, just the ominous beating signifying death.

# SIXTEEN

"STEVE, SIT REP. GIVE US SOME GOOD NEWS."

"Larkin doesn't mess around that's for sure. He took mental and psychological torture to a new level. Almost crapped in my pants myself just watching."

"Spare me the details for the moment. What do we know?"

"Big money, Matti."

"Care to elaborate?" *Any day now. Blink. Blink.*

"Oh, sorry, I was looking at the video feed. This is some messed up next-level shit Matti. Get this. They are the kids of the original scientists. They've been holed together for all these years and were repeatedly tortured to recreate this. Closest they have come is the creation of a fungus-spreading disease in mountain pine beetles."

"Wait, what?"

"Their lab testing has included the creation and infection of pine beetles. You know, the thing that Colorado is famous for. Those beetles are killing millions of acres of the forest. But the intent was more sinister and deliberate than that. Only way to stop it is to remove the trees, or it's breeding grounds for more beetles as drought, overcrowding, etc. makes the areas more vulnerable for attacks. You've seen the carnage. Looks like war-raged country, in some areas, as it's too vast to clean up, with millions of acres destroyed. So, now, not only has it produced a new climate issue, but it's also created a new economic issue."

"Let me guess…It costs too much to clean up the areas, so land gets sold to the private sector. Another virus that was man-made and distributed for financial results."

"Bingo."

"These seven scientists have been together since roughly age eight. They've been repeatedly bound and tortured to recreate what their fathers created, and have had family members killed one-by-one because of their inability. We're talking decades, Matti. At some point, you'd think someone would have said, 'they can't do it, cut our losses.'"

"You must have big money to conceal something like this all this time. More importantly, you must believe it would result in bigger gains to carry on."

"Remember the good Doc in *The Saint*? Yeah, these guys haven't replicated the solution. They'll need three miracles to save them. Someone (or someone's) are full-on desperate, as these guys can barely add two plus two, at the moment, after what they have endured. They are one step ahead of a carrot. I can't imagine how they have survived."

"Make sure Larkin lays off. Eyes on them, but get them outside. Hell, have them play kickball, I don't know. Careful though, as someone has invested this much in them and, deranged or not, they will be looking for them, too."

"What's your next step?"

"Looks like I need to redirect this transport. A bunch of billionaires are meeting up."

"Crap, there's no way. We'd have to drill down on over two thousand. We don't have the time or resources for that."

"Not for this meeting. It's only for the top one hundred, and we can narrow that further down to just those from China, Russia, Middle East, Mexico, and the US."

"Gotcha. Have you told B yet?" he asked.

"Nope."

"Glad it's you and not me."

"Get to work, clock's ticking. And Steve…thanks."

"Don't get mushy on me now."

"You're right. Hurry up, loser."

"That's more like it. Love you, too." He disconnected.

# SEVENTEEN

JOHN D. ROCKEFELLER is the first proclaimed billionaire in 1916. The number of worldwide ten-figure-plus clubs started to explode around the 1970s. You had Friedrich Flick (convicted Nazi war criminal), Adnan Khashoggi (arms dealer), Caroline Rose (hotel heiress), Yoshiaki Tsutsumi (Japanese property investor), and Pablo Escobar (drug lord), to name a few.

Outside of many of them not having names you can pronounce correctly, generational wealth breeds generational wealth. There were only fourteen US billionaires in 1982, but there are over seven hundred today. China has over eleven hundred today.

Now, let's put this in perspective. There are over one point four billion people in China and three hundred and thirty million people in the US. Therefore, when you do the math, the US is once decimal ahead of China. *Use a calculator.* US wealth was generated from cars and technology (still is), while China's richest man today originated from water and tea (big fight for water).

Let's look at the other countries we had in collusion.

Mexico has thirteen billionaires today with the biggest from the telecom sector. The Middle East has twenty-one, mainly from construction. Russia has one hundred seventeen billionaires, with largest coming from steel.

Notice one thing they all have in common? They made their wealth from targeting needs versus wants. Just saying.

Do these billionaire 'play bunnies' impact legislation? At every level. In a democratic society like the US, when government institutions can, unchecked, take away rights granted to the American people, then it's not really the American people who run the country but the whims of government officials with their pockets lined by whoever paid the most. Greed. *I've always stated there should be term limits and we should do away with lobbyists.*

Unless we want to end up like China, where, if an individual expresses an opinion contrary to the CCP, they can't even ride public transport afterwards. We need to be careful of setting up the same precedents.

Know what you and a billionaire may have in common? Divorce. They have the same divorce rates as the average-not-so-rich-or-famous citizen. We are all made for connection.

Bethany and I went from Tel Aviv to Germany to New York to Sun Valley, Idaho. She bitched the whole time. Why Idaho? Well, it happened to be hosting the annual schmooze-fest by bank sponsors hoping someone will drop a few extra hundos (in millions) while you fly fish and strike multi-billion-dollar deals. This event precedes Davos, held in Switzerland, where the World Economic Forum is hosted. China hosts their own version of 'Summer Davos' which competes with the timing of Sun Valley. *I know, big shocker.*

Last time I attended Summer Davos, at the beautiful luxury resort on the edge of Lake Saint Moritz, the Russian counterpart to our Director of the NSA, had his head blown off. Didn't read about that in the papers, did you? Our own corrupt director came to his own demise shortly after. *You're welcome.*

While I was on checking in on everyone's status, Bethany was working on procuring last minute apparel and preparations for obtaining access for our attendance. We would need to enlist help from our friends in DC to pull this off with such a short window.

Despite having visions of pulling up in a Mercedes-Benz 300 SLR Rudolf Uhlenhaut coupe (or possibly a Bugatti Chiron Super Sport 300+), we would be pulling up in a Toyota Camry rented from National Rental Car. We would be bartenders at this event, not attendees. Afterall, it's a small circle in this elite club, and they all knew each other. So, we couldn't show up as newbies in this arena. Per Coughlin's law from *Cocktail...A Bartender is the aristocrat of the working class...*Little known trivia: the movie was based on a true story.

Provided by the resort, we would be wearing black Giorgio Armani single-breasted tuxedo jackets with matching slacks, a delicate white camisole, and hair in a high tight bun with dangly gold hoops. To top of it off we had Manolo Blahnik red leather pumps and matching lipstick. We could have been models for the Robert Palmer, *Addicted to Love* video. Apparently 1989 was making a comeback. Don't kid yourself, just because people have money, doesn't mean they know how to dress or style, despite having paid stylists. Just look at Bill Gates.

At the introductory meet and greet, attendees made small talk and nibbled on Bluefin tuna, Alma's caviar, Pule cheese, gold leaf pizza, or Yubari melon draped with Jamon Iberico de bellota. The patrons came to Bethany and me for their provisions. Namely, we were asked to serve a replicated Ritz-Carlton Diamonds are Forever drink, which, in plain English, is vodka, lime juice, and a one carat diamond at the bottom that we hoped they didn't choke on. *Bless their hearts.* Also popular with the ladies was the 1990 vintage Cristal and also the 1888 Samalery Vieille Relique Vintage Bas Armagnac, which is then finished off with a sprinkle of gold leaf flakes. *Stupid.*

The men were prone to Macallan 55 Single Malt Whiskey, or whatever Bethany and I were serving as we happened to have a bevy of men standing near our station and we were making eye contact with each one. *Remember the divorce rate.*

A group of billionaire stragglers surrounded us as Bethany overhead one of them say "Sweet Cougars."

"Did that motherfucker just call us 'cougars'?" she whispered incredulously. "Needle dick mofos. I see some accidental collateral damage in front of me. Just saying."

*Ouch.* Don't kid yourself, Bethany and I could still hold court with anyone, but it was a reminder that we all have a shelf life when it comes to aging. We could easily pass for fifteen years younger than our actual age. Most of these men were sporting their second and/or third wives that were twenty to thirty years younger. Youngsters who couldn't remember one phone number, nor find a store, without a GPS. That's why they call us when they need something done.

We were there to observe two specific individuals in attendance. Carter Michaels came from generational wealth. His family was the predecessors to the Sackler family in Big Pharma. More importantly, we needed to know more about his ties and affiliation with Vice President Intrator. Second, was Viktor Petrov from Russia. He was hanging with Michaels, and we suspected he would lead us to our KIA.

Carter Michaels looked pervy. No other way to say it. He came across as if fondling himself constantly, with a constant makeshift grin. He was in his late-sixties, lean, brown hair and eyes, with a haircut that said 1970. His initial background was in military intelligence that his parents forced him into, but he moved to the family business and was geared to take over. He had over fifty trips reported to Epstein's Island. Estimated personal wealth at one hundred and fifteen billion dollars. Not including Papa's money.

Viktor Ivanovich Petrov looked like the actor Viggio in the original *John Wick* movie. Of course, many may argue that all Russian men look like that - which would be an inaccurate statement, but just goes to show you how stereotypical one can get. He did have a fat mole in the middle of his forehead that needed desperate removal. Viktor means 'conqueror' while Petrov means 'rock'. Let's don't forget his Patronymic name, Ivanovich. (Son of Ivan...like Ivan the Terrible) He was built like a rock. Late-sixties in age as well. Wore a thick gold chain over his shirt. Guess what industry he was in? Yep: pharmaceutical, research division. Estimated wealth at one hundred billion. *Birds of a feather, stick together.*

Michaels approached Bethany for a drink and pointed at the selection of wines before asking for a bottle of 1970 Chateau LaFluer. Excellent choice and vintage. Although some of the fruit has faded, the structure of it was divine. Bethany remarked that she needed time to decant it and let it breathe, to which he responded with, "It hasn't breathed for fifty years; it's dead. Let's just drink it." Damn, he'd just quoted from *Cocktails,* too.

*Heebee-jeebies.*

Bethany turned to me with her whop-eye and gave me the WTF look. Jetlag was definitely setting in. *Hold it together B, just a little longer.* She obliged with opening the bottle and grabbing two

72

glasses to take to his table. As she set the glasses on the table, she leaned over closer to them and grabbed each of their shoulders. Just under each of their jacket lapels, she placed the microscopic transmitter. Afterall, what we wanted to hear wouldn't be in a public setting. This would have to suffice until we could put more permanent tracking on them.

I said into my earpiece, "Start recording."

# EIGHTTEEN

"HEY, LOVE, HOW'S IT GOING?"

"Glad to hear your voice, finally. The kids are none too happy with either of us that we bolted out of there without them saying goodbye to you specifically."

"We'd be none too happy if they were dead. Did you explain that to them?"

"Think that matters to them?"

"This is all part of the training they're going through. They'll have to accept what they can control and what they can't. When to check emotions and when to understand it's not personal."

"They're our kids, Matti. Don't lose sight of that," he said calmly but with conviction.

"I'm doing all of this *because* they are our kids. They can't lose sight of that, either. I'll sync up with them next. Do we have anything yet?"

"Nothing yet on Michaels and Petrov. The kids are taking turns monitoring with Ainsworth."

"Any progress with Doc's notes and lab results?" I inquired.

"I don't know, Matti. His thoughts were scattered all over. I can only interpret so much before we must outsource it. One thing consistent in his comments is that this new virus has long-term unexplained side effects, and the outcome when you combined the two is anyone's guess."

"What was that meme that came out when it first hit? Oh yeah, *Chuck Norris has been exposed to the virus. The virus is now in quarantine for fourteen days.* Of course, I preferred, *If you need one-hundred-forty-four rolls of toilet paper for a month-long quarantine, you probably should've seen a doctor long before this.*"

"Matti, this is serious. We know you are mutating. We've all witnessed it."

"I love when society preaches 'believe in the science', only to contradict themselves by not following the science. Hell Tom, our nation is so broken we can't even agree on what the definition of a woman is these days. How f'ed is that? Although most of the world would welcome having all viruses vanish, there is an inherent benefit and necessity that we need from them. Most viruses keep us and the planet alive, rather than killing us. In fact, the world would cease to exist without viruses. Although most research has been on pest control, this virus is undeniable for population control. Let me reiterate: the major difference is that neither this virus nor my own virus was natural, but man-made and unquestionably unethical. My virus has a symbiotic relationship with me, and I suspect - due to the longevity and the severity in which others are trying to conceal, procure or destroy –I'm confident that mine will prevail…and you can tell Chuck there's a new *Walker, Texas Ranger* in town."

"You need help," he responded. "We, you, need someone on the outside we can trust; this is beyond our scope or expertise. This is an elevated *Bourne Legacy* experiment."

"Probably his best movie. He was hot in that one. Of course, there's no comparison to you babe. Jeremy Renner was genetically enhanced. I was genetically created…Love, I wish we had someone we could trust. For our kid's sake, for now, we are on our own."

# NINETEEN

I BROKE A PROMISE. I promised my children I'd never leave again without saying goodbye in person. There are inherit risks with this profession that are understood, but neither I, nor them, ever expected I'd be gone for a year due to a mission gone wrong. It changes you, and it changes the ones you love. There's blind faith and trust, but there's also abandonment and fear. My concern for my children (and for the nation) was a forced conforming based on fear of continuing to treat the symptoms and not the problems.

When the kids told us they wanted to follow in mom's footsteps, I had the same reaction that any normal parent would have. I thought, "How badly have I fucked up my own kids to protect America at all costs?!" It took a hot sec to come to terms that they are my DNA.

Not to mention, the triplets were born on 9/11. Triplets just like my brothers and me. There are signs everywhere. Sometimes we must look back to see them.

Each of the kids had their own natural and individual abilities that allowed them to excel. Not bragging, but all three were lookers. That's not what made them stand out. Matthew was a fluent linguist in multiple languages with a strong disposition towards history. Strategic warfare and intelligence were his strengths. Mary excelled in business processes and was a fearless leader. She would be Command. Mark was a physical specimen in his own right, and our religious compass. He'd be the brute force: the frontrunner into any physical situation.

The training program would hone these skills while also mastering a barrage of other areas: weaponry, logistics, warfare, and physical conditioning, to name just a few.

Our training program also incorporated what we called the 'human element'. You can't do this line of work without serious repercussions on the psyche. I mandated that this be the main derivative from the training program: the skills they needed for survival in life. We wouldn't be replicating a Liev Schreiber scenario in *Manchurian Candidate.*

Two words children never want to hear from a parent...*I'm disappointed.* The same two words a parent never wants to hear from their children. I've been beaten, shot, tortured, and done the same (and more) to many of my adversaries. I feared more hearing these two words from my family.

No time like the present: time to rip off the Band-Aid.

Only one ring, and the first words out were "We haven't forgotten, Mom, that you broke a promise. Just as you have told us, you are only as good as your word and your integrity."

*DAMN.* Without saying 'disappointed', the word was said. The downfall of group face time, where I could see the disappointment in all their eyes at once.

"My loves, I'm so sorry. I didn't have time to explain when we initially called from Nola's. I know Dad later explained the situation and the high risks and concerns involved. I'm still working on this parenting thing. You know, there's no manual for this. My intentions are always for your safety first. I won't allow someone to get to me by using you. I couldn't handle that..."

Mark, the more light-hearted one at times, broke the ice. "There's no manual to get to the mess hall, either. Just saying. You should have at least texted with an apology; we would have understood. Don't you think? You didn't even mention it in your call."

#proudmommymoment quoting *A Few Good Men*. As parents, we are often our own worst critics on how we parent. Learning is a two-way street.

"Roger that, baby. I hear you all, loud and clear. In case I don't tell you enough, you all are always my first priorities. How are the fatheads by the way?" *Deflection time.*

Mary, our confirmed dog-obsessed kid, was quickest to reply. "They really need more exercise, Mom, and Mark needs to stop giving them extra treats. Especially to Scully."

"With this extra free time away, why don't each of you feel free to take them out more?" I gently offered. "You all would have loved seeing Koda and Bruiser on a HAHO jump."

Each of them was quick to respond simultaneously with, "What? Why do they get to do all the fun stuff? Are you kidding me?"

*Shit. My bad. Probably best for now to leave out the part about the plane exploding...*

"I've been a little busy juggling multiple balls in the air. I'll fill you in later. So, do we have anything yet on Michaels and Petrov?"

Matthew was quick to add, "I translated messages from Petrov. We've isolated a potential location on our Russian 'uncle'. He's outside the border of Ukraine. Mom, they're the ones that tracked your plane. They were trying to set Renat up."

*My brother. So strange to think of my brothers after all these years. Crap, Ukraine of all places. God have mercy on him if he was involved.*

"Send me what you have. I'll need to review it and get with Bes and Lily."

"Just sent to you. Already sent to them, and Matthew is working with them on logistics. They are waiting on your call," added Mary.

*How's that for Command?*

*Let's do this* by *Outskirts* came to mind... *Are you ready for a comeback? Are you ready to fly? Are you ready for the moment? Get ready to ride...*

# TWENTY

FAITH IS TRUST OR CONFIDENCE in someone or something that is without proof. Personally, I had the Russians involved in two assassination attempts and being connected to my brother. I had faith that Bes and Lily would be able to resolve it. I've seen them in action. I wasn't putting faith on the fact that it would be resolved peacefully.

"Bes, give me some good news."

"Well, if you thought my cousin was bat-shit crazy before, be glad you're not with her being pregnant. I pity the fool that crosses her." He answered in his thick accent.

"You've been watching way too much American TV to quote Mr. T from *Rocky III*."

"Your TV is much better than ours."

"That's not saying much. Anyways, let's have it."

"Your kids sent over the info from Petrov. Freddy sent over what he obtained from DC. You do realize that Russia is roughly two times larger than the US, right? Just FYI. China is same size as US. We're looking for needles in multiple haystacks."

"So, are you telling me you have nothing? Wait, why are you referencing China here?" I asked.

"Just wait. What I'm telling you is that we should be considered gods, with what we've accomplished so far. Lily tracked down and is in route to gather intel and take care of your 'friends' who sent your KIA and same group that tried to take you out over Tel Aviv."

"I'd say they were incompetent. How's China involved?"

"You know that enemy of my enemy is my friend shit? Well, we can confirm it's Petrov who has been orchestrating it all, but your SAM was produced in Russia. That doesn't mean shit though as it could have been sold and repurchased by anyone. Petrov is definitely a player, but we're also digging down to see if China is using Petrov and your VP in a misdirect. That's why Lily offered to 'gather intel'."

*Christ.* "Any closer on tracking down my brother?"

"We're narrowing it down. The man is a mechanism for sure. Missing a chip, in that one. He's left a slew of carnage all over Moscow, did some serious damage in Manchuria, and appears to be heading closer to Ukraine now."

The Russian invasion of Manchuria occurred in the late 1800s, when China was defeated by the Japanese and Russia realized they needed to up their efforts if they wanted any expansion efforts. Manchuria was important region due to coal and mineral deposits. The Japanese carted prisoners of war in WWII by 'hell ships' to tend this area as slave labor. Had they not occupied this area, they wouldn't have been able to carry out more of their attacks on the US and British Empire. The region was quickly divided between China and Russia. Sounded like someone(s) didn't want to share anymore.

With the escalation of the Russian invasion into Ukraine and China's perceived political necessity to reacquire Taiwan, it warranted a response from the US. That's exactly what both countries wanted. They are playing chess while we are selectively playing checkers.

"Once you set him in motion, he will not stop. I can relate, at times. Who's giving Renat his orders? Putin? Or do you think he's flipped?" I asked.

"That's the interesting part. It appears he's gone rogue. We're trying to connect the dots on his victims. I'm bringing a team with me to place a net."

"Bes, we need him alive. He has his guard up, even more than usual. Fear causes hesitation and hesitation will cause your worst fears to come true."

"Wait. Isn't that from *Point Break*? Damn all those 80s American movies were so good."

"Close. It was early 90s whippersnapper. Vaya con dios pero con mucho cuidado."

# TWENTY-ONE

HUMAN'S NERVOUS SYSTEMS are not designed to experience extended states of survival mode. In fact, it makes us sick physically, mentally, and emotionally. I'm the rare exception, not the rule. The pandemic and the government-sanctioned requirements of masks, vaccines, boosters, travel, and what-nots had prolonged this heightened state way past any expiration date.

Which government agency was designed to keep our country safe? Ironically, the Department of Justice (DOJ). Composed of US Marshals, the Bureau of Alcohol, Tobacco and Firearms (ATF), the Drug Enforcement Administration (DEA), Federal Bureau of Investigation (FBI), and the Federal Bureau of Prisons (BOP).

The DOJ reports to the Attorney General, who is appointed by the President and confirmed by the Senate. In laymen's terms, the Attorney General is the highest officer in the country. They advise the government on legal matters, that happen to be raised by the president. So, you have someone with over one hundred thousand agents at their command to pursue fugitives, pedophiles, drug trafficking, terrorism (domestic and international) and prisoners. *What a motley crew.*

There is another little independent agency of the US government that seemed to be on everyone's radar after this little pandemic virus started. The Consumer Product Safety Commission (CPSC) pursues the safety of consumer products by concentrating on "unreasonable risks". They oversee developing uniform safety standards and conducting research into product-related illness. Now, why would this agency be completely free standing? *Blink. Blink.* Created in 1972, it reports to Congress and the President.

Pharmaceutical companies were reporting breakthrough infections and were now promoting booster shot number gazillion with reports of monkeypox as a cover story to 'allegedly' conceal vaccine-induced herpes. No one wants to hear about the big H. Monkeypox sounds like a better cover. *WTF.* World Health Organization Chief declares a worldwide public health emergency, advising same sex partners to avoid the viral disease. Why is anyone falling for this? Willful ignorance. It's easier to blame someone else than to have accountability.

It's an easy check. Find out how many congressmen/women have had (any or) multiple boosters and serve on any committee with direct contact to any of these said agencies. They haven't or have stated they have had four boosters and still caught the virus (multiple times). You can take that bet to Vegas. Don't need to be a rocket scientist to do a checks and balances on this.

My missions had multiple run-ins with many US and international agencies and countries ending in 'A'. Although a staunch advocate for our country overall, that doesn't mean you should neglect the checks and balances afforded to you. The only agency to date that I had no issue or conflict with directly was the FBI. That was changing. Then, again: their greatest counterintelligence arrest was in 2010, when they arrested ten Russian illegals after they detained Anna Chapman, whom they deported back to Russia where she would head up a youth council, be a catwalk model, and star in a television series. *Not to mention, the FBI f'ed up Nacatomi Plaza in Die Hard. If only they had called me to handle things...*

Although it's a popular notion that the Vice President of the United States simply provides public appearances to represent the President, constitutionally, the Vice President of the United States primary role is to be President of the Senate. They have no vote unless it's a deadlocked vote, and it shouldn't be surprising that the Vice President has had to intervene on a tie-breaking matter almost three hundred times since 1776. There've been twenty-three ties that needed intervention just this year. That's equivalent to eight percent in one year alone. We are not united, but a house divided.

I had a secure direct line to the President; he answered on the first ring. "I was expecting your call. How are you Matti?" Borrelli was always sincere, but also personable. His ability to navigate on so many levels was impressive, and I had to appreciate that he let his hair down (so to speak) with a little drum playing when time permitted. Presidents are people, too. Why anyone would want this position in these times was beyond my ability to process. You either had to be a complete patriot or complete narcissist. Most likely a combo of both, but Borrelli was the last of his kind.

"Outside of a little jet lag from some world travel and someone blowing my plane to pieces, I can't complain."

"I'm glad you're ok. I was briefed on an unidentified object blown over Tel Aviv. We did our best to deflect any knowledge or participation. Wasn't hard since we didn't know. So, do you know who wants you dead?"

I laughed. "Where do you want me to start?"

"Fair point. How can I assist?"

I liked that about him - direct and to the point. "I need to know if there is anything up for a vote that's not been publicized yet?"

"Interesting timing. There are small rumblings about rolling up the Consumer Protection Agency to another department."

"Which one?"

"Well, they tried rolling it into the Department of Commerce during the Reagan era with no success. I would have expected the FDA under Health and Human Services, but by all preliminary accounts they are targeting DEA."

*DEA is under DOJ. They regulate the manufacture and distribution of controlled pharmaceuticals; including those used by researchers to conduct studies. Basically, you must be licensed to administer them. Enter Michaels and Petrov...GREED.*

"Do you think your VP is compromised?" No point beating around the bush.

"I don't, but I can see the scenario you're setting up in which he may be used unknowingly." *Ol' Pres catches on quickly.*

"It appears we both have a lot of balls in the air right now. Put your big boy pants on, Easton. We need a president that will lead."

"Matti, thanks for the heads-up. Watch your back. You know how to reach me if you need anything," he added.

"You'll be hearing from me. By the way, I need a new plane."

He could be heard laughing as he hung up. *Guess he thought I was joking...*

# TWENTY-TWO

"WE DON'T HAVE ANYTHING ON Intrator that we can pin to the KIA," is how Freddy started.

"I didn't think you would. After more consideration, I think they wanted us to waste our time and resources pursuing that, versus another agenda," I responded.

"What do you have? I have some theories too."

"Intrator has been too bogged down with the current Speaker of the House, and Congress with impeachment, insurrection, and conviction testimonies. Let's not forget: the only thing that has minimalized it was the fact that the past Speaker (who was filling in for our MIA Pres and VP) blew her own brains out at Command Center. Otherwise, it would be a witch hunt for Borrelli and Intrator. They have utilized technology and social media to their benefit, and should be thankful their press secretary is a fucking rock star versus the previous administration's incompetent idiot."

"We are on the same wavelength, then. They were hoping you'd take out Intrator."

"Bingo."

"Per the 25$^{th}$ Amendment, if the VP was no longer able to serve for whatever reason, the President with the approval from Congress, would fill the vacancy. You're not implicating Borrelli now, are you?" he asked, speculating on my reasoning.

"If this came to fruition, after everything that has transpired, he wouldn't be able to bring in who he wants. There's plenty of folks who still want him impeached, despite him operating in the best interest of the country. His hands will be tied. I think he'll be offered up an independent as the best solution."

"Does this independent have any ties to a country that ends in 'A'?" he inquired. *There's, like fifty, that I can think of off the top of my head.*

"Let's hope we don't get to that. As of now, you, Sedlin and Long need to reinforce protection by whatever means for Borrelli and Intrator…for team U-S-A, you know that other 'A' country."

"You getting any rest?" he asked like a typical parent.

"Barely. I swear I'm like John Travolta in *Phenomenon.* I'm sleeping less and less every day. Processing faster and faster, too."

"We need the team to focus on your medical concerns, Matti," he pleaded.

"It's on my radar, I promise. I'm not doing all this not to be here. We may have a necessary Plan A exit for all of us when this is all over."

"Kiddo, you're not Ryan Gosling in *The Gray Man* either."

"Don't get me started. I saw that on the transport back from Tel Aviv. Taxpayers' dollars at their finest. Sure, he looked hot, but come on already. He took out three teams while handcuffed to a rail and then still managed to get into the building without anyone noticing and retrieved the kid. Puh-lease."

"I recall not too long ago when you took out a team of thirty back on the ranch…" He trailed off.

I smiled momentarily. "True. That's because I planned and had help, and not this pure fiction over-the-top bullshit. I just hope some hot, up-and-comer plays me in the series. I already have the tagline, 'Freedom comes at a cost and the payment is Matti Baker and her team,'" I added teasingly.

"That would be some academy award-winning acting they would need to pull off, but it's a pretty accurate tagline."

"I agree. Thanks Papa."

There was an unexpected silence on his end. I probably only have ever called him Father, Pops, or any other affiliation to being a parent maybe one time before. I had my aunt and uncle, who took me in and whom I considered my adoptive parents; and then I had Freddy, who had also always been there, and who'd shielded and protected me all my life.

After a moment, he offered in a choked response, "Thank you, kiddo."

"No, Freddy, *thank you*." I hung up the phone in fear of my own choked response.

# TWENTY-THREE

LILY WASTED NO TIME in collecting the members that organized the two attempts on my life with our KIA and the plane bombing. She was like a hound dog able to sniff out the tiniest of morsels. There were six team members - well, before the one ended up dead on the side of a mountain.

I watched on camera as she had them secured by chains from the ceiling. How she managed to get five of them tied up like Sylvester Stallone and Kurt Russell in the prison scene of *Tango & Cash* is anyone's guess. Although she was just starting to show, I must admit, I winced to witness a pregnant woman enjoy inflicting pain like this. It was unsettling.

Sweat drenched from their bodies, hair slicked to their heads, facial expressions in defeat from shock and awe, these five were facing pending death – and they knew it.

Lily would torture them individually while the others waited in vain and then look would back at the camera intermittently, seeking from me any indication to proceed or stop. They'd attempted to kill me twice. Stopping would not be coming from me.

No amount of training and can ever prepare you. You just want the pain to stop. You can't think anymore. They understood they were past the point of survival, evasion, resistance, and escape. There was only death. The question that remained was for what. For their country? Family? Loyalty? Greed? This answer would determine how long the torture would endure. There is always a breaking point.

Lily took her time. One by one she continued with the torture. She had slipped and they tracked her to the airport in Naples. She would give vengeance. After hours she was able to pull together and confirm that the KIA was sent only to take Chanlor out in efforts to get my brother to resurface. *Interesting. Their main mission had nothing to do with eliminating Chanlor's DNA makeup.* The solo woman on the team was selected and sent based on her precision marksmanship. How did she miss? Was it really an eagle that intervened? *A miracle...*

On the other hand, when they targeted my plane, it was to eliminate and blow me to smithereens across the sky. *Why not at the compound? They needed to ensure they had me and the vials together? They didn't realize I had the vials on me at the time. They must eliminate those as well.*

Lily continued torturing them until we could confirm the biggest pieces of the puzzle. Who funded and ordered the hits? Why did the Russian brother go rogue? One by one, she was merciless until there was only one remaining. The others had bled out from her tactics, but she was patient with this one. Intuitively, she knew that his one would give her what was wanted. *You just want the pain to stop.*

He begged, pleading for it to be over. He preferred death. *Please just tell her what she wants, and this will be over.* Lily took him down from the chains and cradled him in her arms. This was her final act. In an almost dream-like trance state, he told her it was Petrov and Michaels who'd funded it all, and the brother went rogue as he contracted a virus, and that it had a hostile, unprecedented effect on him. He, too, was regenerating, but with adverse effects. Their solitary mission was to destroy; never to conceal.

Lily took her hand and wiped the tears from his eyes, while she gently moved his hair back in place. She brushed her lips over his forehead, and in her final act, she snapped his neck. There would be no more pain for him.

The last hour of events had the Steve Miller Band's *Fly Like an Eagle* on repeat in my head…*Fly like an eagle, let my spirit carry me, I want to fly like an eagle… Time keeps on slippin', slippin', slippin', Into the future…*

# TWENTY-FOUR

I CALLED JAKE.

"Jake, we need the location of Chanlor's father, and I'm talking yesterday."

Jake had taken Chanlor back to Texas as he coordinated tracking down my brothers. Chanlor's mother was relocated from Washington DC to San Antonio, Texas. San Antonio has four major military installations. In addition to the military bases, you had warm weather and the affordable cost of living motivating civilians, military, retirees, and veterans to this city. With over one and a half million in population and being the seventh largest city in the US, you also had a large canvas to hide someone(s).

"We are monitoring the nursing facility twenty-four seven. No visitors, or calls. Nothing yet. Since the pandemic broke out, the facility requires reservations for any guest or outside admittance. Not that he would go in the traditional way, but if he opted for a concealed cameo, he would need to make an appointment. There is a reservation for a woman in fifteen days. States it is for a medical physician follow-up that is not provided through the facility. This could coincide with timing of their last visit. I'm cross checking with any new or pending lodging, car rentals, etc, but we have a big area to canvas with surrounding cities."

"I'll be there. Jake, our top priority is him. Not the wife, not either of the daughters. They want to destroy, not conceal. He's been out on his own, now, too. He doesn't have any government backup anymore. He may be physically or mentally compromised.

What do we always say?" I inquired.

"I know, Matti. Desperate people do desperate things."

"How's your girl holding up?"

"Finally, out of the fog. No thanks to you, but she's resilient. She's anxious, but that's to be expected. It's not like she's been trained for this."

"Hey, now, I didn't have a lot of options at the time," I countered. "It was either dose her or leave her to be killed. You're welcome". Switching subjects quickly, I added, "How's the backup for Bes? Does he have a team together for what he needs?"

"He's good to go. Countdown twelve hours. We have you set up in a similar fashion as with Lily where you can watch, observe, and intercede remotely. Steve and Tom will be handling the drone surveillance."

"I'll reach out to Bes immediately and remind him that our mission is to protect. At all costs. Jake, be careful and keep Chanlor close…for her safety."

"Roger that."

# TWENTY-FIVE

MY CONVERSATION WITH BESSUM WAS QUICK. A gentle reminder that this was my long-lost brother, and we were there to not capture, but contain for his safety. We needed to obtain additional data on this mutating genetic make-up of us three. Individuals and countries had been killing for decades to secure this information.

But it wasn't to conceal or contain anymore; it was to destroy. Why? What if the three of us had genetic markers that if recreated, allowed individuals to self-heal? What would that do to the health and pharmaceutical industries? They would collapse. No more diabetes, no more cancer, no more anti-depressants, no more long-term prescriptions. No more dependency. Governments and big business don't want that.

China was quickly becoming the world's largest pharmacy overtaking the top five that currently resided in the US and European markets. There are two main stages to the pharmaceutical supply chain – you have active pharmaceutical ingredients (APIs) and then the formulation process that puts these ingredients into that little pill, liquid, cream, etc. China, along with India, source up to eighty percent of the APIs imported into the US. India saw significant increases over generic drug formulations that no longer held patents and are open to any country or company to produce and sell, but they also now rely on China for APIs. Our Defense Health Agency argued 'the national security of increased Chinese dominance of the API market cannot be overstated.' No one listens. Why? *Greed.*

China's weapons of mass destruction may just be those: of using the collection of human information along with genetic makeups to make us dependent on them for the long term. It is never advisable to be dependent on your government (or, especially, another country).

With any dependence of the global pharmaceutical supply chain, if another health crisis occurred, China could hoard access to any other nation. Especially now, with mounting tensions over Taiwan.

Why were such extensive and costly measures put in place for myself and my brothers? The potential outcome of eugenics or a CRISPR methodology would have a devastating financial impact. In eugenics, you have the racial improvement or planned breeding, and it could be theorized that certain demographics and races fare better when you can eliminate socials ills through genetics and heredity. CRISPR would offer new solutions through gene editing. Combine the two and you better start practicing your Mandarin. *Ni Hao.*

It appeared that Renat, was indeed a reborn man on a mission. He was tracked from Moscow to Ukraine and was now headed by all accounts, to Shanghai – the other side of the continent. Why Shanghai? It was the top location for Chinese billionaires located on the central coast: one of their largest cities, and a financial hub. Adorned with skyscrapers and major attractions, it was a tourist dream destination. It captured an American fascination thanks to movies like *Indiana Jones and the Temple of Doom, MI-III, Pacific Rim,* and pretty much most Jet Li films.

And, with over twenty-eight million people, it would be almost impossible to track. Almost. We were isolating individuals tied to the largest pharmaceutical companies. This narrowed our search to two adjacent buildings. Having recently seen captured video and still pictures of my brother, he had a combination of Keanu Reeves and a younger Mel Gibson look and air about him. Renat, Jardani (or whatever his name was) was good-looking, tall, and lean but muscular with short black hair, but he possessed the same eyes as me. Dark blue irises, with flakes of yellow and translucent blue in the middle. We certainly shared and possessed something distinctive.

I was conflicted thinking that I may meet my brother today. After all these years, it was surreal. I found myself not giddy, but on the spectrum of hopeful. *I was not alone.*

As with most parking in large downtown areas, parking would be in the lower garage levels of the buildings. Bes had teams secured in both garages. He had himself positioned in the far east building garage, as there were two billionaire pharmaceutical CEOs in this building who happened to be on location that day for a joint meeting. Bes deduced that they were the target for Renat based off his recent activity.

We had cameras and full visuals in place on both sites. Steve and Tom were monitoring the outside with additional drone coverage. Freddy was on satellite. Bethany was with me as we scoured through every individual that entered and exited the building and garage. The meeting was scheduled to adjourn at 3PM. It is twelve hours ahead of us since we had touched down in DC to reestablish additional provisions after the airplane debacle and set up monitoring for Lily. We now directed our attention and initiatives to Bes.

"Hey, snacky-snack time?" she asked.

"We're fifteen minutes out, you'll have to wait. Stay alert, they won't be late." I responded incredulously.

"I'm starrrrving," Bethany blurted with a Cheshire cat grin.

Bethany was habitual stress eater. We'd be on missions in the crucial moments and if you had a bag of nuts, cookies or chips or anything else laying around, consider it gone. I ate for fuel provisions; she ate as a consumer and worshiper of food. It never interfered with the timing or the outcome, but there was always chance for a first.

"It could easily be thirty minutes or longer. I have time to grab something."

"Are you kidding me right now? You do understand that in the Chinese business culture, when a meeting is finished, you are expected to leave before any counterparts. Leaving late is a serious offence."

"They are billionaires. They pretty much make up their own rules and standards by this point, don't you think?" she retorted while she scoured through her bag looking for anything to eat, but only finding gum.

Killing me smalls. *Breathe in, breathe out.*

The hairs on my neck were tingling, indicating that something was amiss. I scanned through all the screens; it was eerily silent. We were missing something. Visions of Keanu in John Wick were flashing through my mind, telling me something ... *Whoever Comes, Whoever It Is, I'll Kill Them! I'll Kill Them All!...*

"Anyone have eyes on Renat, yet?" I asked hurriedly.

Individually, Steve, Tom, Freddy, Bessum all signed off with "negative."

"Bes, pull out. Pull both teams out now!" I commanded.

"What? Are you kidding?"

"Pull out and double time it, Bes. Get as far away as possible!"

Bethany looked over to me quickly, trying to figure out what I was calculating, while keeping eyes on the screens. The tensions mounted as the clock ticked closer to three. You could feel something brewing. The clouds outside were getting ominous, collecting, and getting darker by the second. Droplets were now falling. A storm was coming, and its name was Renat.

We were in the rainy months of Shanghai. Umbrellas were going up as the water fell. The added coverage that he needed. How could he had predicted this? *Please, Bes, get far away.*

We watched as a motorcade was coming down the street, entering the garage facility one by one. Six black, armored vehicles in total to escort out our two targets. We watched as they circled down to the lower garage level floor for the select and discriminating clientele. One by one, they came to a stop. It was 2:59.

"He's there. Check all the staircases and elevators, look for any movement coming out of a car on that level. He may have been there this whole time. Bes, are you at a safe distance?"

"Roger that. Not sure why though. We had two capable teams in place, Matti."

"Keep traveling, you need to make more distance."

"Tom, Steve – anything on the outside?" I barked.

Tom replied, "There's nothing unusual yet, Matti. Just a flock of birds circling the east building in this rain."

"Did you say birds?" I felt gutted asking.

"Yes, at least twenty."

You don't see a lot of birds in China. The Chinese government launched campaigns against birds in 1958. Mao dictated that birds be killed over the grain they ate, to bring better hygiene to China. The Great War, so to speak, that they eventually lost out on. How ironic to lose a war against a sparrow, a symbol of love.

The clock turned 3:00. I silently held my breath, closed my eyes, and prayed for a brother I have never met. *Don't be afraid; you are worth more than many sparrows.* I opened my eyes in time to see the elevator doors to the lower garage level as three armed personnel and our two targets behind them exited. They were quickly joined and flanked by additional personnel as they proceeded toward the armored vehicles.

3.2.1.

Across from the motorcade, a car trunk opened, and Renat jumped out of the unsuspecting vehicle, which had been previously cleared. A long, black raincoat flowed and scraped the ground as he moved closer, approaching the vehicles.

"Matti, it's him!" Bethany exclaimed. "We need to send Bes back in and get him."

I turned to her and calmly stated, "He's not coming back." And with that, we heard, then witnessed, the explosion that made everything go black.

*He just wanted the pain to stop.*

*DEFCON II.*

# TWENTY-SIX

WE ALL WATCHED and sat in shock and attempted to process what we had just witnessed. Immediately, Tom pinged me privately. "Babes, I'm here for you. I love you."

Bes was first on the open comms to ask, "What the hell just happened? We could feel it all the way down the street."

Freddy took the lead in filling him in while we waited to see what structural damage was done as the smoke billowed out in force. Visions of a 9/11 repeat of the twin towers loomed subconsciously in the back of our minds, predicting that, if one tower fell, the other would, too. People were running and screaming in all directions as the rain continued to fall, heightening the fear and uncertainty in everyone.

I stared at the screens that now only showed black. A missing piece, as always, in this never-ending puzzle. Why now? What triggered this escalation? How could I have changed the outcome? Would he have done this if he knew I was here? Did he care? *I'll never know.*

"Steve, where is Petrov?"

"Give me a sec to isolate," he responded as he quickly hacked away on a keyboard, then came back with, "We don't have eyes on him anywhere."

"B, rewind and put up the last footage of them exiting the escalators," I instructed her.

"Got it. Three armed personnel in black suits and baseball caps are with them."

"Zoom in on the middle one," I said as I watched the screen and came in for a closer look.

"That's as close and clear as I can get it. You can't see the face in the middle with the hat on. He knew to shield it for any cameras."

I shook my head from side-to-side as I looked closer. "We don't need to see the face. Look there at his shirt," I said as I pointed to the screen.

Bethany turned to me and said, "That damn piece-of-shit gold necklace. It was Petrov. How did you know?"

"I was trying to think of why he would do it for just these two. Looks like Renat took out two from China and one from Russia," I stated flatly.

"Must be that triplet bonding, telepathy stuff they always talk about," she added, referring to me knowing what Renat was thinking versus the three dead.

*Hmm.* Triplets can be identical from the same egg, or from three eggs being fertilized, or a dizygotic pregnancy, where one egg divides into two identical fetuses and the other egg does not. The chance of having triplets is one in ten thousand pregnancies. Of course, we were our own special odds. The old wife's tale that twins or triplets have a special bond from birth that will take them through life. We were separated at birth with completely different upbringings socially, environmentally, and economically. The only connection we shared was a dead mother. *Abandonment.*

"Freddy, take over command. Bethany and I need to get to Texas pronto. We need to map out a new game plan. All, let's circle back. Tom, I'll reach out when on way to airport. Love you, babe," I said as I clicked off my mic.

"It's 4:15AM. I think you need a minute after everything that has happened. I mean, damn…" She then added, "just how do you think we are getting there, anyways?" Bethany inquired with her right eyebrow slightly raised.

"There's this new thing where you can rent nice planes from private airports. Maybe you've heard of it," I answered, deflated.

"They sell planes there, too," she smiled right back.

"No time for that right now. And, for the love of God, I'm working on something. I need to take the dogs out. Be ready. Doors open at 7:00."

"Sweet Jesus, I hope it's a beauty." She turned to walk to the other room, humming John Denver's *Leaving on a Jet Plane.*

# TWENTY-SEVEN

WITH THE EXPLOSION OF THAT MAGNITUDE, guess how many news outlets had reported it in their early morning news segments? Zero.

There are essentially six companies that own almost all of the US media: National Amusement, Disney, Time Warner, Comcast, News Corp, and Sony (yes, a Japanese company). So, with twenty-four-hour news outlets, internet, newspapers, etc., what are the chances that not one was reporting that two of the largest buildings in downtown Shanghai had an explosion and three billionaires were no longer walking this earth? *Holy mother...*

Shame on anyone if this comes as any surprise. Companies such as Google and Facebook have ongoing pending anti-trust lawsuits on the delivery of accurate information in the wake of the mounds of misinformation disseminated after the pandemic. There's no question that they colluded in their messaging, timing, and opinions, and 'allegedly' benefited by providing agencies millions of dollars in free advertising. Why? Eyeballs were glued to their sites, which in turn leads to more ad dollars. *Ka-ching. Greed.*

Each of the owners and/or CEOs of these organizations are also billionaires. Just saying. Collusion is defined as a '...secret or illegal cooperation or conspiracy, especially in order to cheat or deceive others.'

Collusion is not always considered illegal, especially when it is mandated by your own or outside governments and agencies. This happens all the time…for the good of the people. *Cough, cough.* The New York Stock Exchange was founded in 1792. Although there have been brief interruptions or halts since its formation, the big notable closures happened after: Lincoln was assassinated; railroad bonds; WWI; the 9/11 attacks; the 2008 housing crisis; and 3/9/20 with the pandemic declaration.

The Securities and Exchange Commission's role is to enforce the law against market regulation. They are also another independent agency just like Consumer Products. *Blink. Blink.* Over the last two centuries, they have implemented a set of qualifications for a halt to occur, beginning with a decline of seven percent of the S&P 500 for a first halt, followed by thirteen percent triggers for a second halt, and finally a twenty percent decline for a full hard stop.

Let's put it into another perspective…what do you think would happen to the market if three billionaires were assassinated by a major explosion in a highly dense city of twenty-eight million impacting two of the richest buildings in the world…market halt and/or crash? Sure, you and I would feel it, but who would benefit from it? Who else can buy when the market is low? Other billionaires.

Despite it lasting for decades, Renat played the short game and, in the end, paid for it with his life. I needed to work the long game to protect the American people…even if it was against themselves.

# TWENTY-EIGHT

I CALLED TOM on our way to the air terminal. "You get any rest babe?" was the first thing out of his mouth.

*Who has time to sleep?* "I got a few after I took the dogs out. I'll get some rest when we get to Texas."

"No, you won't. Talk to me, love."

*Where do I start? Why is it so hard?* There's a reason most people who are in this line of work are single. You can't afford the distractions. In my case, I couldn't allow anyone to use my family against me. What ending would you choose for a loved one? Harrison Ford (aka President Marshall) in *Air Force One,* or Michael Nyqvist (aka Viggo Tarasov) in *John Wick?* Outside of the big man upstairs, if it was your spouse, child, or best friend, can any human really adhere to the needs of the many outweigh the needs of the few, or the one?

When faced with a situation one will instinctively fight, freeze or flee. It's in your DNA. My DNA was genetically enhanced. I would always fight. For my country, family, and friends. That's what scared me the most.

"Tom, we need to have Ainsworth take the kids and meet back up with Larkin for the time being. You and Steve will need to come to Texas for reinforcements."

"You think they have tracked David?"

"I think there are billions of reasons why they would. If we can finally locate him, so can they. They'll bring an army, so to speak.

Probably in the evening, hoping to get a two-fer with me."

"Then let him go Matti. Live to fight for another day and time. It's too risky."

"He's on his own, he has no reinforcements, and he's been cut off financially. I'm sure he has been following everything, and realizes. I think he's coming as he can't abandon her," I trailed off.

"She's already gone, Matti. She's not there. He needs to let go and so do you on this."

"I can't ask him to do what I couldn't do," I said softly.

"What is that?"

"Abandon my family. I'd rather be dead than alive, and I know he feels the same."

"Matti, you do see the irony, right?" he stated, understandably agitated.

"I'm the only hope he has left. A sister he has never met. They'll continue to target our loved ones to get to us. I can get him, Tom. I know I can with your help, and we'll all figure out together how to unleash this to the world."

"Again, this isn't *The Saint*. This is real, but if anyone can do it, I know it is you," he affirmed.

"You always did like Elizabeth Shue in that movie," I teased.

"You're the only green-eyed lady for me," he teased back.

I'm not sure how many years it took for Tom to know the true color of my eyes. Granted, I wore brown contacts when I met him and had a multitude of disguises for my missions, *but really*...

Thankfully (for me), he changed subjects. "Hey, I forgot to mention, but did you know that Ainsworth writes, plays music and an is an artist, too?" he stated to me quizzically.

"Really? Who knew, a damn renaissance man." I laughed.

"Oh god, don't call him that. It would surely go to his head. The kids jokingly call him Jesus, since he let his hair grown out. He borrowed one of Mary's hair thingies on the last road trip and I thought she was going to flip out," he laughed.

"Lord, help him," I joked. "It will be good to have the kids with him and Larkin. Semper Fi."

"Oh, they are faithful alright. Craziest Marines I have ever met. Maybe they should be the ones meeting us in Texas?" he added

"If Armageddon is coming, I want them with the kids. Plus, I need you to pick up some provisions on the way down here. We need to increase our stockpile after FAB. I'm talking the big guns baby."

"Don't sweet talk me like that, it's been too long," he baited.

Smiling, I responded, "I'll holler when we touch down babe. I love you, Tom."

# TWENTY-NINE

WHEN WE ARRIVED AT THE PRIVATE AIRFIELD, Bethany was practically salivating when she viewed all the large jets. I'm sure visions of the next conquest were running through her head. I may have failed to mention to her that I had already checked inventory and she was not going to be thrilled with the selection. I had only moments before her storm was going to hit.

"Which one is ours?" she asked excitedly.

"Um, well, it's over there," I said as I pointed in the general direction.

"What? Those are all the small aircraft. Do you mean over there to the right of them?" she questioned as she pointed in a different direction towards the Falcon 8X and Global 7500.

I walked up to her and turned her face in the direction of our selection as I pointed. "See that white and red Cherokee 6 300? That baby is all ours."

"I fucking hate you," she deadpanned.

"There is nothing wrong with this beauty. They didn't have anything else available. Plus, we're flying low. We need to keep under and off any radars," I replied with a big smirk.

"Koda, Bruiser, your mommy doesn't love you," she directed to the dogs in a higher-pitched voice. "Look at their faces, they hate you too."

"Make out a flight plan. We'll need to stop on the way, as this doesn't have the range," I added.

"Like you need to tell me that. I have visions of that Ron White bit of the plane crash...*we got passed by a kite...we lost some oil pressure...if one of these engines fail, how far will the other one take us? All the way to the scene of the crash...*"

We both laughed. We seriously need help.

# THIRTY

FREDDY WAS BUSY NAVIGATING and coordinating with multiple agencies after the Shanghai FUBAR, while also trying to ferret out who, if anyone, we could trust to help us. It was slim pickings, to say the least.

Although we personally never had previous issues with the FBI, no one ever believed they were on the up and up, either. Let's face it: their mission is to protect the US from terrorist's attacks. How could they not be involved in any of this? They have had their share of controversies starting back in the 1980s with the unauthorized installation of national security devices on American citizens. Let's not forget what happened in Waco, Texas with a fifty-one day nationally televised siege that ended with the Branch Davidians compound being burned to the ground with everyone in it. Of course, my personal favorite was Ruby Ridge. Remember that nugget? A former factory worker turned survivalist got in a shootout over…wait for it…his failure to appear in court over weapons charges. His wife and son were killed by federal agents, and he received a little over three million of hard-earned tax dollars. You can't make this stuff up. There's plenty of material for a documentary series. Just saying.

We were bringing a war to Texas. There were six of us versus who knows how many they could or would bring. We were tracking

David, and we knew they were tracking him and now us. As careful as had been before (and we still mis-stepped, at times), we were purposefully leaving footprints so they would locate us. It was simply a matter of time. We could solicit additional private military security, such as Blackwater, but their deep ties with government contracts and their own nepotism would bring more long-term problems than solutions. With the loss of Petrov, we were counting on Russia using the Wagner group to come after us, a bunch of de facto private army members (aka mercenaries). The same group that they were using in their war with Ukraine. A war that was supposed to last six days was still going almost a year later.

I debated contacting Aldo. The Italian mafia has affiliates in the US, mainly in New York and Los Angeles. Of course, the FBI was tracking them, too, and selfishly I needed Aldo to protect my aunt and uncle and keep them as far away from all this as possible. Let's not repeat the Alamo, right? Reminder: None of them survived. *Probably wouldn't hurt to have him call in a few favors...*

Freddy pinged me on a secure network. His face looked tired. I felt like his face.

"I sent you over the schematics for the facility," Freddy started. "It's over ten acres, with one main gated entrance and one road to the community center that then splinters out like fingers. They have over one thousand residents at various levels from independent living to assisted living to full nursing care. She should be residing in the full nursing sector, but she was admitted as fully independent, with twenty-four hour round the clock care."

He paused momentarily, "How you are holding up after Renat?"

"Probably faring the same as you. For someone I never met, I was looking forward to finally meeting him. It would have been

112

nice to compare notes, but more importantly…," I started to trail off. "…I guess I wanted to just touch him, as weird as that may sound. To feel his physical being and to know it was real and we were in this together."

"That doesn't sound weird at all. I was hoping for the same thing."

"Do you think we are fooling ourselves? If they can get to him, they will continue to come for us. This pandemic reinvigorated their hunt for us, especially me."

"Being isolated was his Achilles heel. You are surrounded. We just need to stay one step ahead," he replied with a slight twinkle in his eyes to give reassurances in a grim situation. "How do you plan to draw them out? We don't want to have Armageddon on the premises."

"Working on that ol' wise one. Tell me, can Sedlin or Long contribute anything to this?" I asked.

"They're one step away from being out. Even if they were willing, I don't know if they would jeopardize it. Being capable is a whole other convo. They asked me to help them on their Bumble profiles. Though, there is one angle that they may be able to assist that I need to flesh out."

"Did you tell them to start by putting up a picture other than themselves?" I laughed. "Surely your new gal pal, Erika, has some single friends that can help them out?"

Freddy was briskly rubbing his forehead back and forth before he answered. "Little too early for that ask and I've been a career solo. Not sure I'm ready for it, myself. Luckily, I have distance working in my favor right now."

"Don't be stupid, Freddy. You're over thinking this. Go grab the girl and make her yours, and after you do, I'll be sure to take all the credit," I teased.

"That alone is enough to make me not want to contact her again."

"We're all made for connection," I added solemnly referencing back to the previous convo.

"You've been the exception, Matti; certainly not the rule."

"It's time to change those statistics, Freddy. Carpe diem."

"Can we talk about something easier? Say, nuclear fusion or how are we going to approach the site?" he deflected.

"Check your phone. I just sent over something you could possibly use."

He pulled out his phone and tapped. "Picture of The Three Stooges. Funny, Matti, funny."

"If you screw it up with her, you can add your bio to Sedlin and Long's pics. Just trying to be helpful…" I mentioned as I put my feet up on the desk.

"Shoot me now. Please," he offered before closing his laptop.

# THIRTY-ONE

"I THINK THE KIDS may have stumbled onto something. Again," Tom told me while I was jotting down some notes to myself.

"That's great. Let's hear it."

"They went back to the crime reports from Doc's lab. As to be expected, firefighters were first on the scene. From their individual reports, each stated they had never seen an ignition like this where it almost caused a back draft and incinerated everything down to the core until it was obliterated. Their statements were that it was 'next-level incineration.'"

"So, we have a combo of Backdraft and Iron Man 3 in the making?" I asked.

"Exactly, and here's the kicker," he added. "Just like in Iron Man, the kids have tracked identical circumstances to two other locations, as well."

"Hmm. Let me guess. One is probably at one of Michaels' lab facilities, the other oversees at a testing site?"

"Just once, I'd like to surprise you." He sounded dispirited.

"Well, I don't know exactly where, but I'll take an educated guess. One was in or near DC and the other in Wuhan, China," I remarked.

"You can be irritating, at times."

"Babe, circle back on the truck report and see if there was any unknown chemicals or accelerants noted. Maybe they micro dosed it as a test run? Just check, please. Love you too. I'll get back with you," I promised as I hung up.

Like US prison systems, you have your run-of-the-mill testing centers and then you have your maximum-security levels. Wuhan was the now the epicenter in work for the world's most dangerous pathogens, and was also the alleged culprit for the start of the pandemic. There are four biosafety levels, with BSL-4 being the highest level. A level 4 infection has no known treatment and high fatality rate (i.e., Ebola).

The US has only four labs at BSL-4 level, with the main one in Atlanta under the Center for Disease and Control. In total, the world has only fifty-nine such sites operational to date, with twenty-five in Europe. China's ministry examined and approved up to four more at level four and almost ninety at level three. And they had operationalized to build more despite the 'alleged' controversy. *Greed.*

To date, there is still no confirmation of where the virus originated despite numerous reports and tests, but an ongoing storyline that it remained an open investigation. Over six million people's deaths were attributed to this virus. It takes money to conceal at this level. Big money.

I miss the days when the news told you when to think about something, versus what to think. With news channels and social media now providing their opinions versus sharing information, and even blocking accounts that shared anything contrary, it was understandable the confusion, anger and mistrust the public was experiencing was understandable. Again, your involuntary processing intake when a person feels threaten is to fight, freeze or flee. Unlike myself, the majority seemed to be going for the last two options. With extended time alone or in the home, birth rates in the US saw a small increase for the first time in the last few years after being on the decline. Don't get too excited, as it's still almost half of what it was not even forty years ago. The sins of our parents, per say, would transfer this genetic makeup to this new generation. Not only would it be DNA transfer, but the environmental and social factors that were created and withstanding. Masks were still being worn despite all conclusive evidence that they made no difference. It's like TSA at the airport, providing security theatrics but contributing nothing. Fear is a terrible thing to live with.

What could cause such an incineration? There are things you simply cannot incinerate - activated carbon, is one example. Characteristically, solid wastes must be heated for up to ninety minutes while liquids and gases require only seconds. The explosion at the lab was instantaneous, yet even bone fragments (per the reports) were almost undetectable, and all other traces of incineration non-existent. They had no conclusion as to what had ignited this. No follow up was ever announced or communicated publicly.

In 1986, the Chernobyl nuclear power plant in Ukraine had a catastrophic malfunction in reactor number four and it took over ten days to extinguish. It was only discovered because radiation made its way to Sweden. The truth was kept from the public and it took over ten days and hundreds of firefighters to quench, with many losing their lives. The emissions continued for weeks, and radioactive clouds spread as far as Norway. Recently, Russia attempted capture of the largest nuclear plant in their war with Ukraine, with reported radiation levels emitted by twenty-fold.

Ukraine is similar in size to Texas, which only has two nuclear plants. Ukraine has fifteen plants total, so you can understand the global severity of any war on the country.

Once again, without confirmation of sources, we are left to ask what is the cost of lies? And for me, I ponder what has potentially been created and dispersed on American home soil, taking the phrase 'leave no trace' to a new level.

DNA tracing began in the late 1970s as scientists understood the potential for identification and biological relationships. It's now commonly used for the identification of dead bodies, or in burn cases. DNA is no longer traceable after exposure to temps over one thousand degrees Celsius, or eighteen hundred and thirty-two Fahrenheit. The levels of fire range from deep red, orange-yellow, white, blue, and violet which is recorded at three thousand Fahrenheit. The temperature of the core of a nuclear reactor can be as high as forty-three hundred and fifty Fahrenheit.

Why was I obsessing about this?

I was born in 1976.

# THIRTY-TWO

PHARMACEUTICAL COMPANY LOCATIONS are like Home Depots and Lowes. They predominantly reside right beside each other as they compete for your dollar. In the US, you'll see a CVS by a Walgreens, a LabCorp beside Quest… yadda, yadda, yadda.

Washington D.C. had a bevy of who's who of pharmaceutical companies and their subsidiaries. You have Pfizer, Merk, and roughly twenty percent of all pharmaceutical companies located in the Washington, DC area (almost four hundred). In fact, what one may consider 'pharma road' is located roughly two miles from Capitol Hill. Real estate is king, baby.

The DOJ is less than a mile from Capitol Hill and the DEA headquarters is three miles down the road from them. Michaels had his company located right between them all, just on the other side of the Potomac River, closer to the DEA. Again, real estate is king.

The whole thing with Renat occurred so fast, we didn't have time to truly comprehend the ramifications of what it meant on a global scale. My brothers and my genetically created, now mutated virus, was a worldwide ticking nuclear bomb to the pharmaceutical industry; an unforeseen anomaly that they could never have forecasted. Originally created with the objective to distribute, we were now targeted to eliminate. Michaels would not stop with Renat.

I do so enjoy old songs and movies. They seem to resonate with me, but more importantly, they act as my own psilocybin therapy without having to take shrooms. There are treatment centers now popping up all over the world promoting the benefits of these 'magic' mushrooms. No pun intended. MDMA was the rage in the '80s and '90s. It was outcasted in the early 2000s. Now, it's being promoted as the 'it' drug to help with breakthrough therapies. Don't forget how hydrocodone/opioids got its big promotion... 'breakthrough infection'. Advertising gurus don't need to change the slogan, as it continues to work on the willed public.

The Human Health and Services Department, along with our pals at the FDA, would have to give approval. With marijuana now legalized in nineteen states and more states legalizing each year, Big Pharma and Big Tobacco are marketing high-potency THC products. Billions of dollars are flowing into this new industry of smokable, edible, and drinkable products. Health care officials are reporting psychotic episodes and are saying marijuana has now become a hardcore drug. So, one needs to think of the next big thing to monetize. Welcome back, Ecstasy...

Recreational, health care, military, and all kinds of applications emerge to counter the other legalized and approved drugs that your momma never saw coming.

I flipped through SiriusXM channels before falling on John Waite's, *Change...We always wish for money, We always wish for fame, We think we have the answers, Some things ain't ever gonna change...*

Why do you think Jeffrey Epstein's infamous list was not publicized? Who was he friends with? It's always about money, our new DEFCON.

There are signs everywhere. Will it stop you or drive you is the question. Oh no, make no mistake for me. Just like Wyatt Earp in *Tombstone*, it's not revenge I'm after. It's the reckoning. When past misdeeds must be punished or paid, and when the degree of one's success or failure will be revealed.

I was thinking bigger than what was going to go down in Texas and that it would be felt by many more than just Michaels.

# THIRTY-THREE

JAKE HAD ARRANGED a provisional compound on the outskirts of San Antonio. The whole team was finally together again. This brought me comfort and also angst, as the stakes were even higher, and the children were not with us.

Dating back to the Roman Empire, families would often not travel together to a destination in the event of a catastrophic circumstance. By horse, carriage, car, boat and especially later with planes, you'd see the mother and father split the family up as they made their way to their final destination. I always thought this was perplexing. Afterall, do you want to leave half of your family behind to deal with the aftermath of the other's demise? Is it simply preserving a legacy? Is it worth the costs? Or is it a parent's instinct for survival? Or revenge?

While Jake was setting up the tactical operations center with the assistance of Freddy, Bethany and Steve took a moment alone to regroup. Tom and I video chatted with the kids and were also afforded some much-needed time to discuss our own family preparations. "I don't like that we are both here without the kids," Tom started.

"I have the same reservations. I wanted to get your thoughts before I instructed Ainsworth."

"I just can't see the end game as clearly as you. How can we compete against a decades-long bottomless money machine whose now singular mission is to eliminate you and your brother at all costs?"

"We change or divert the mission," I stated matter-of-factly.

"And how are you going to go about that?" he inquired with peaked interest.

"You've heard of Tam Jackson, right?"

"Jackson, the former romance author turned political influencer?" he asked skeptically.

"The one and only. What have both political parties been notorious for in election years?" I paused just momentarily before answering myself. "Misdirection…we'll need to use the media to have our adversaries focus on a new issue. One that will be close to their hearts."

"I'm missing something. You think a former romance writer is going to sway overnight money-making conglomerates to change directions?"

"Have you listened to or read any of her stuff? She's a freaking rockstar. She's also a staunch activist with over one hundred million Twitter followers. She'll follow the trail we'll provide and more importantly, she'll report it accurately. A new tide will be imminent. They'll have their own new mission that they'll need to pursue."

"Won't that be just temporary?" he added.

"That's all we need for now." I placed my hand up high and then lowered it and repeated, "with me, or without me?"

"Holy shit, you're really quoting *Knight and Day* right now?" he asked, incredulous, but with a smile on his face.

I smiled back and grabbed his hand.

"With you," he stated as he led me back to another room.

# THIRTY-FOUR

---

## Monday

WHEN BETHANY APPROACHED the conference table, she had a solemn look on her face that I wasn't sure what to make of…at first.

With over thirty years of friendship, we had been through it all. Training, single days, covert missions, marriage, births, deaths, and a slew of bad men she had devoured. The hairs on the back of my neck were rising, as I realized I had seen this look many times before.

I pulled her aside and just came out with it. "What's happening?"

"Steve and I decided it's better if we aren't 'together, going forward," she said, with air quotes, and was straight forward with her response.

"Really? Why now?" I was asking, but more questioning the timing.

"We played it out and it was going to happen at some point, so we'd rather it be sooner versus later. I'll always love him, but I'm not in love with him."

"What happened? Is there someone else?" I asked.

"No, nothing like that. He needs and wants someone to take care of. I'm not looking for that at this stage of my life."

"Yeah, that sounds horrible: to have someone who wants to take care of you for the rest of your life. I can see why you don't want that," I stated with emphasis.

"Quit it, wench. After we're done here, Jake will be by himself again. Steve and he can resume where they left off. It's better for everyone this way," she added.

"Did I miss something? Are you implying they are together?"

"Ha – oh, hell no. Well…I don't think so." She laughed with her head cocked. "No. It's all good. It was the right thing and time to do. We didn't want any additional distractions; we have too much at stake, right now…for all of us."

"You sure you're ok?" I asked with a sincerity in my voice.

"I'm good. I know I always got you, my Day One."

"Don't get any ideas," I said with a smirk. "Ok, let's do this."

We walked back to the group and sat down to discuss the logistics of the next one hundred and twenty hours before the projected arrival of my other brother. Steve looked across the table at me and gave a quick nod of his head and a reaffirming smile. He was going to be ok. He was a trained Navy Seal, after all, but my heart still ached for him. *We are all created for connection.*

As we looked over the diagrams, we had a daunting task with only six team members. We had to have eyes on the entire perimeter, inside buildings and inside the wife's personal residence. Brother David would be in disguise escalating our isolated efforts. Not only would we need to identify him first, but we had to retrieve him before our enemies did. There's a fine line between passionate and crazy. You can't reason with crazy, and we weren't taking chances that they wouldn't blow up the entire complex and all of us along with it.

We hashed out a slew of possibilities and probabilities, each bringing their respective skill and experience to how we could best accommodate the mission. The chief concern was that we were operating on a lot of assumptions. And, you know what assumptions means, ASS out of U and ME. Or, simply put, FUBAR.

Jake and Steve both referenced their outside experience with Operation Red Wings. In 2005, despite cross departments best intel, Operation Red Wings saw the demise of eight Navy Seals and eight US Army special Operations aviators. The mission was to interfere with local Taliban efforts in attempts to provide regional stability before parliamentary elections. They were ambushed by the Ahmad Shah.

Crazy is what we were also dealing with, with even less intel. Worst case scenario - they send in the Wagner group with intent to burn the entire place to kingdom come. Plan for the worst, hope for the best.

After grueling discussions, we collectively agreed that the best course of action would be having Freddy as our drone surveillance, Tom and Steve would be perimeter with the dogs, Jake would be on the building rooftop, Bethany would be back-up and transport and I would be inside long beforehand. We had our own version of *Ocean's Six* going on, but we also wanted to ensure that there was more than just one *Lone Survivor* at the end.

"I think we're set then." I looked to Freddy and added, "We're counting on Sedlin and Long coming through. Do we have confirmation?"

"Let's hope our calculations are correct on timing. It's either going to be way off or really tight," he responded.

"That's reaffirming," I mocked. I scooted my chair back and stood up. "Let's get this party started. B, meet me in thirty to prep. Tom, let's go call the kids and Ainsworth. He'll need time to coordinate with Larkin, so we need to get a move on. Steve, what are you sending us out on?"

Steve was scrolling through his Spotify list before he landed on *Holy Grail* with Justin Timberlake and Jay-Z. He fast forwarded to the lyrics… *And we may never meet again, So shed your skin and let's get started…*

Although a great and powerful beat, the mood turned ominous in the room as we walked out to start our respective duties, with the others wondering if he was forecasting our demise and myself concerned that he was struggling and was really focusing on Justin's chorus…*One day you're screaming you love me loud, The next day you're so cold, One day you're here, one day you're there, one day you care…*

Either weren't good options.

# THIRTY-FIVE

## Tuesday

IT WAS 5:20PM when the emergency alert was triggered for medical attention in Unit 1004 in the high-rise portion at the facilities. By 5:31PM, a fire truck and ambulance were admitted onto the campground and quickly ascended to the residence. The front desk was notified that both the resident and elderly caretaker were being admitted for medical evaluation for stroke and possible anxiety attack. An additional gurney was brought up to the residence to take the second patient. In under thirty minutes, two patients were wheeled to the emergency vehicle and whisked away.

Within thirty minutes, the four EMS personnel consisting of Jake, Steve, Tom and myself were able to deposit and conceal a M134 and McMillan TAC-338A sniper rifle onto the rooftop of the high-rise, bring in a bag of Remington's 700CP rifles, and a shit-ton of monitoring equipment, grenades, tranquilizer darts, and disguises...all the while transporting out two civilians from Unit 1104 one floor above the call in. Three personnel exited the building. It was between the second dinner rotation accommodating half the residents and the 7:00PM shift change. No one was the wiser.

# THIRTY-SIX

## Wednesday

I HAD THE ENTIRE EVENING to stealthily move throughout the extensive complex as the retirement, nursing and memory care residents were sound asleep. The occasional housekeeping crew did not question me as I departed from the back entrance with my bag of gear in a trash receptacle to go about the premises. Labor was still an issue in this and every industry as they strived to bring in additional personnel to perform the most basic duties. The excuse of supply chain management was rampant, as many couldn't or wouldn't resume after the pandemic. *Not every industry was waiting on a chip from China.* Disgraceful as you saw the elderly taken advantaged at every angle. The turnover rate in this industry afforded me the luxury of being neglected.

Security cameras were aimed for front gate, inside the main entrances and elevators. They weren't looking for someone breaking in, but a resident breaking out. Dementia, the cognitive decline of many of the aging tenants; a daily reminder of the cruel aspects of aging. I was dressed in the same uniform as housekeeping and, once off the main campus, had free roaming for the most part. I went quickly, setting up various strike points.

The temperatures were sweltering even at these late evening hours. As much as I loved the great state of Texas, I remembered why we moved out of this miserable, God forsaken heat. Just happy we weren't in Houston with its higher humidity. I was making mental notes, as we needed a new residence at the conclusion of this mission. If we made it out alive.

The residence of Marie, David's wife, was a sprawling two-bedroom apartment on the top floor with two separate balconies off each bedroom. One for her and one for the twenty-four/seven caretaker(s). The view overlooked a cascading pond and fountain that provided a false semblance of cooler weather, as it overlooked the city skyline. He spared no expense for her well-being as it was decorated to the nines. She had a help assist chair off her private balcony and in the main living room. Walkers adorned the bedroom and entrance. The kitchen was small in comparison as residents in the main building were escorted to the main lobby dining hall or the other dining options for rotating meals with their friends and guests versus the rigors of cooking in their domiciles. Marie had no family or guest's visits. The facility's motto was: *A place where friends are reunited, dreams are achieved, and life is lived to the fullest.* Another reminder we have failed this elderly generation and that one day I'd be joining their ranks. I prayed my kids never had to take care of me and that I had my mental and physical faculties until the end, but statistics were not in anyone's favor. What would my mutating virus turn into? There were no stats on that.

A white board in the small dinette area off the kitchen listed a weekly calendar of appointments. Marie had only one appointment scheduled for Friday at 10:00AM, a routine time for a doctor's visit or checkup.

The contract agency had already been notified that there would be a change in schedule this week with "family" in town and their services not needed until Saturday. Sadly, no one questioned that. It's simply a paycheck. Meals were scheduled to be delivered to the door versus going to main dining hall. Unit 1104 would be overlooked.

There were no family pictures on the wall, nor on her nightstand, nor anywhere else. Nothing that could tie her to David or her children. What a lonely existence for preservation.

I called Bethany to verify her arrangements. "How'd it go? Any problems?"

"If I didn't know better, I swear her eyes indicated she was aware. You could tell she recognized Chanlor when we got her back here. There was an instant relief that you could sense. Chan completely broke down. It had been years since she saw her mother. Marie can't talk - not sure if she can even hear - but her eyes are expressive; like she's still in there, like…she knows."

"B, she needed hope. She's been through enough," I said in a choked response.

"Damn, Skippy, you don't need to tell me. Nothing is happening to this woman while we have her."

"How's Jake?"

"He saw the reaction. He knows what's coming. He understands." she responded.

"Love you B. Get some rest. Just like the rapture, the countdown has started. We just don't know when."

Defcon III.

# THIRTY-SEVEN

## Thursday AM

EVER WONDER HOW military missions get their names? A few of the most notorious were Operation Overlord, Anthropoid, Downfall, Rolling Thunder, Barbarossa, or Wrath of God (my personal favorite, in naming rights only). *Operation Enduring Freedom may have been a naming faux pas...*

Why is mission naming even a thing? Well, Germany started the shebang during WWI to maintain secrecy. By WWII, countries really started to get creative. Not only were they created to maintain security, but also contributed to motivating the troops. Winston Churchill was credited with coming up with a higher level with degrees to naming rights. The US now uses a computer system, NICKA. It tracks previous codes, names, and activities, so no duplication occurs. Commanders at the highest levels are tasked with naming rights, and there is a whole hellavua mess with multiple steps. Military at its finest.

As a private contract operative, I didn't need to adhere to the same protocols, but I was a staunch advocate for this exercise as I felt it did aide in the general morale of the crew. Unlike military mottos... *This we'll defend, Fly, fight, win, The only easy day was yesterday, Semper Fi, Semper Supra*...mission names were to pertain to the particular situation at hand. Without the use of computers, three-step verification process, or any other outside contribution, our group voted unanimously in a matter of a mere ten seconds on the mission's name of "Operation FU." *How's that for efficiency?*

In 2008, the Russo-Georgian War lasted six days and was recorded as the top ten shortest war. It was a Russian victory occupying South Ossetia. Over two hundred twenty civilians were killed and over five hundred injured. *The Russian-Ukrainian war on the other hand...*

There were three stages to Operation FU. In simplest terms, the first phase was the successful exfil of David, his wife, and his two daughters. The clock had already started, and the total projected timeline was under five days. Stage two, the decimation of Micheals and a few notorious others. Anticipated timeline, one day. Yep, one day. Go big or go home. Third, the semi-permanent relocation of our team. Timeline, two days. So, eight days max. How many injured or killed would be determined by how many they sent.

Bes and Lily were together in Sicily and video conferenced me to check in and see what the status was and if there was anything that they could assist with in the interim (aka, anything they could be paid for...). Apparently, Sicily is the vacation city to go to for all the locals. Leave Rome, Florence, and Venice for the tourists. Never had a chance to visit Sicily myself. I would need to see how I could rectify that in the future. Bes's son was participating in a jiujitsu competition at the tender age of eight and he was elated, telling papa stories of him easily taking down the opponents. Pregnant Lily was revealing a softer demeanor as she experienced the changes of pending motherhood. She beamed when I inquired about the sex of the baby and told me it was a little boy. He would be a mafia king in the making.

"Have you considered a name?" I inquired.

Her head ticked slightly sideways as if she considered me an idiot for even asking before incredulously stating, "His name will be Price, after his father, of course. That is customary."

Looking at the screen, she detected the half smile on my face, before adding, "Oh, you thought it was someone else's. He's the head of the Sicilian mob. You don't think he can arrange conjugal visits in prison?"

I visibly laughed out loud on that one. That's not what I was thinking at all, but best not to irritate or instigate a pregnant woman. Plus, Aldo, Tia, and my parents would be joining them shortly for an extended period. I wasn't about to enrage her hormones.

Bes winked and signed off with, "See you on the other side." *Not sure if he was referring to the Apollo 8 mission or the Ozzy Osbourne lyrics?* Hmm. We really needed to get him a new hobby.

The next call was the one I was dreading but couldn't put off any longer. One, two, then three rings, and finally Jake joined on Facetime.

"Hey, everything ok?" he asked.

"Just checking on you. How's Chanlor doing with her mom?"

"Her emotions are all over the place, understandably. Happy, elated, scared, confused…she's not sure what to think, I'm sure. We're working on the arrangements for when we successfully get her dad and sister and them all together."

"Love that optimism," I smiled. "But more importantly, how are you doing?" I asked sincerely.

"I'm good, Matti. I wouldn't ask her to stay after she finally gets her family back together. There're too many uncertainties going forward. It just wasn't meant to be, I guess. Not my time. At least, not now."

"Jake, you can always go with them when this is over. This could be your time." I replied.

"No. I made a commitment to our team for at least four years. Plus, with Steve now single again, I can't break up the dynamic duo," he said, trying to lighten the mood.

Trying to rein it back in, I responded, "Jake, this is one of those commitments that no one would question if you broke. Everyone would understand."

"Remember what Annie said to Jack in *Speed*?" he asked.

*"Relationships that start under intense circumstances, they never last...*You do realize...that's just a movie." I replied.

"Movies have a funny way of showing you the truth at times. Listen, I'm good. You don't need to worry. Plus, I already helped Steve set up his new dating bio," he added trying to quickly change the topic.

"Oh, good lord. God help us." I laughed. "What's with this generation and swiping right? Just go out there and talk to the person."

"Listen, at his age, women dismiss him since he hasn't been married before nor had kids. Crazy as it sounds, they'd prefer to have someone who has been divorced versus never married. But, don't you worry, I think I already found him someone to take the away the sting of Bethany."

"It's been like, what, three days?" *Holy shit!*

He was quick to dismiss my comment, and added, "Her name is Annette. Looks like a good, wholesome gal. Just his type."

"We're out of here in three days, want to rehash that Speed quote again?" I stated with my eyes wide open.

We both laughed on that one.

"I'll be on the rooftop in a few. You think they'll come knocking early?" he asked.

"If it was me, I would have had the team set up there already. Oh wait…I did." I continued, "Let's hope they underestimated, picked an inept group, or can't regroup with the curve ball we are throwing their way. Either way, be prepared. We'll be bringing in our newest version of *Thursday Night Lights*."

"*Clear eyes, full hearts, can't lose.* Gotcha back, Matti. Always."

# THIRTY-EIGHT

## Thursday Noon

"WE HAVE AN ETA YET?" I asked Freddy.

"In route. This is quite the feat if we can pull this off," he replied.

"That's why they come to us. Keep me updated. I need to work on some other prep. Over and out." I signed off.

We had peppered enough crumbs for Michaels to want to come after both David and me in one fell swoop. I was going after his vanity, the favorite sin according to Al Pacino in *The Devil's Advocate*. Regardless of if he was using The Wagner Group or any other contract mercenary group, their plans would be to breach the facility. We were counting on this. Our plan was counter intuitive; we were branching out. You can't reason with crazy, and sometimes you just need to join them.

Just over two hours northeast of the retirement residence was Ft. Hood, Texas; the largest active-duty Army base in Texas. Sedlin and Long had pulled some major strings in their final culminating act. Sedlin, being the former base commander, was a serendipitous benefit to the request. Ft. Hood houses over three hundred tanks and hundreds of other support vehicles. They were also experiencing an unprecedented number of publicized accounts of soldiers' deaths, sexual assaults, and drug allegations. They needed a positive PR boost badly, and that's what we were providing. We enlisted our new pal, Jackson, to aide in our efforts.

As part of a goodwill gesture, a military convoy was in route to the many veterans that were residents at this facility to commemorate and celebrate its one hundredth year in operation. A military convoy can be as little as six vehicles or ships. After WWII, the largest convoy occurred in Colorado, with over twelve hundred vehicles and sixty-four vehicles and over five thousand soldiers. We weren't going for a Guinness record here - we simply needed twenty to make a sizeable presence and provide a false cover.

There are organizational elements to consider for a convoy of any size: formations, distance, time, identifications of vehicles, placement, safety, etc. Not to mention who was ultimately footing the bill. *That would ultimately be American citizens.* Even though the distance was just over two hours normal drive time, this endeavor would be considerably longer in duration to move over twenty vehicles.

Preferably, I needed them here before the 5:00PM local news time and, more importantly, the start of the first dinner shift. I silently prayed that no vehicle would break down, causing any disruption to the timeline.

Now, in full disguise as Marie but with a concealed bullet-proof vest underneath, I took the walker and slowly opened the balcony door to let myself out and sit on a wrought iron chair. The left side of my mouth drooped, and I dragged my left leg as I shuffled onto the balcony. I had my left hand in a permanent fist, just like Marie. The chairs were more for stability than comfort. The location of the chairs and outdoor plants allowed me to be seen, but not in an easily accessible shot range for an average sniper. Not that either would provide any barrier. Unfortunately for me, it was mercenaries, plus David, that would have me under surveillance. Therefore, admittedly, I was a little skittish about a head shot. Mercenaries would have no problem shooting in broad daylight, but they would relinquish their primary objective in doing so. If they were already out there, I was hoping for intelligence, surveillance, and reconnaissance only at this point.

David could be just as likely to shoot if he recognized Marie was being impersonated. I stared blankly out at the horizon just as she had been doing since her arrival. Careful to mimic her with little to very slow movements, my eyes suddenly teared thinking of the silent hell she must endure day in and day out, with David watching from afar and not being able to do anything.

I just sat there with no movement. My eyes eventually closed as I soaked in the sun. My mouth still pulled downwards, my left hand on my lap crumpled. I was daydreaming about our birth and life, intertwining fact with fiction. Wondering what life he had undergone. Was it like mine? Better? Worse? He also had found love and family. Though, Renat's life was totally different. All parents wonder and question this with their own children. Same upbringing but totally different outcome. Why? How? What changed? Or was it simply due to manufactured, manipulated, mutated genetics?

Over the years, I often wondered what our given names by our mother would have been. Jardani, Renat…would his life had been any different if he grew up as John or Jason? Was I supposed to be Taylor or even a Shelly? Certainly, my fascination with names started at an early age due to this.

In our small but distinguished circle of specialists, Renat was known to be the leading expert in counterintelligence and explosive devices, evident by what he'd accomplished in Shanghai. The world was shocked, then elated, when the towers didn't fall. David was hired for his stealth and special reconnaissance; and me - well, for superior processing speeds and unconventional warfare. *Of course, we were all proficient in sharp shooting.*

Long ago, I understood and even appreciated what Mom sacrificed for us and our country, despite still struggling with how she got there in the first place. As I've repeatedly told my own children, once you move the line, you will eventually step over it, and it will lead to self-destruction at the most basic level. As a society, outside factors have infested our primal instincts; to react to dangerous situations in the interest of self-preservation. Mom operated under the false pretenses to preserve the US and Renat, and David and I may share in the same inkling and fate. Renat had already met his.

I was still staring out to the horizon when something caught my eye. I didn't move, I didn't flinch, I didn't wink. *Breathe in, breathe out.* I waited. Then, slowly, ever so slowly, I clumsily maneuvered out of the chair and made my way back inside to uncertain safety. It was game time.

# THIRTY-NINE

"THE PARTY HAS STARTED. Freddy, verify count." I voiced over on secure comms.

Jake was concealed and in place on the rooftop and was already lamenting about the heat escalating. Bethany was transporting Chanlor and Marie before her return, while Freddy was pinging satellites to ID drone location of our unwanted visitors. Tom and Steve needed to time their arrival with the convoy and were standing by with Koda and Bruiser in tow. Looking at the monitors, Jackson and her crew had just arrived and were already at work directing people and setting up cameras. On open channels, I overheard local news channels flabbergasted that they weren't in the know, and they were sending their own crews in hopes to catch in on the action.

A large crowd would be imminent. Just what we wanted. The front guard quit stopping cars to enter when he was instructed by the front office after learning that an unexpected military convoy was stopping on their premises as a special surprise to their residents. Jackson had used social media to alert her followers, romance, and political activists alike, who started to come and line up in droves outside the premises.

Aging residents throughout the property started arriving in anticipation of seeing the main attraction. Many in fine physical shape were joined by others in wheelchairs, walkers, and/or with their family or trusted caregivers to give a helping hand. This would be their highlight for the day, month, and for some, even years.

"Four teams – one on southeast corner, one on southwest. Two teams appear to be in movement from same locations but are slow due lack of concealed opportunities and unanticipated disruptions," Freddy announced.

"Eyes on them," responded Jake.

"Tom/Steve, sit rep?" I asked.

"Calvary coming, less than one mile away, and we've successfully tagged onto their heels," Steve said enthusiastically.

"B, what's your status?"

"I'll be coming in hot and providing the coup de grace at 222mph when I'm given the go," she said.

"It's 'gras', but ok, whatever," I said.

"No, I meant it how I said it. They'll be begging for grace," she laughed.

One by one, the vehicles entered with five reconnaissance jeeps, five cargo trucks, five HUMVEE's, and five M1117 Armored Security Vehicles to close it out. The M1117 carries a MK grenade launcher and a M2HB Browning machine gun. It's fricking badass.

Right now, we figured that if they were American contractors they were wondering "WTF...Screw this" and if Russian (or any other country), they were thinking they weren't in the market to die like Gladiators and let's bug out.

As the residents 'oh and ahhed', four of the M117's slowly made their separate ways to the four corners of the property line escorted by a jeep, truck, and HUMVEE in tow. Deliberately, they took their time. Taunting our rivals. One convoy leg stayed at the main lobby entrance, and residents were now also greeted by two good-looking soldiers handling military trained elite German shepherds who were making the rounds while secretly checking for any bomb explosives on site. Who doesn't love dogs? *One of the soldiers was more handsome than the other, in my opinion.*

"Freddy, do we have confirmation of ID on any others? Hate to throw a party without the main guest…"

"Nothing yet. We anticipated a crowd of a thousand. Between the retirement community and Jackson's super followers, we probably have closer to three to four thousand."

I had given David a perfect window. Was he hesitating or did he not understand the invite?

Five minutes, became fifteen, which became an hour. The residents were visibly exhausted with the second shift starting to head to the dining hall. We couldn't have the whole crowd leave, or this would be all for naught.

I sat in the recliner now positioned towards the front door…waiting. Vacillating between a prayer and hearing the words of *Wild Hearts Can't Be Broken* by Pink running through my head… *I will have to die for this, I fear there's rage and terror and there's sickness here, I fight because I have to, I fight for us to know the truth…*

As I repositioned my HK P30L under my lap, the door opened to the face of a woman.

# FORTY

---

ANIMALS AND HUMANS ALIKE have innate instincts, the ability to respond to certain stimuli, and an inheritable tendency to elicit a response. For humans - denial, revenge, loyalty, procreation, and greed shape but also threaten our existence. *Greed.*

Renat, David and I were billion-dollar malfunctions. We were created and militarized so they could send us on missions they instinctively knew were wrong. They sent us because we didn't exist, but they relied on us wholeheartedly. We were created for destruction. Even the best plans go awry. They failed to factor in my mother's instinctual DNA.

I recognized the woman who opened the door. Eyes are unmistakable in color that is unique to every person. There are miniscule differences. No two people have the same eye color, and but there are similarities you can't ignore.

Before me, I saw eyes as distinctive as my own, with dark blue irises, amongst flakes of yellow and translucent blue in the middle.

David gave Dustin Hoffman a run for his money with a full-blown *Tootsie* transition, albeit a bit taller. He looked exactly like the care giver that we gave time off for the week. I was still disguised as Marie, the conflicting images we both displayed.

We had waited a lifetime for this moment. I didn't even know about him until later in my life, but I always knew I was lacking someone, something, in my life. A phantom body part missing that you ached for; longed for. I lost out on my chance with Renat, so I did the only logical reaction. I ran towards him with open arms, into an embrace that whole-heartedly hugged me back. It was nirvana.

# FORTY-ONE

"HOW DID YOU KNOW I WOULD COME EARLY?" he asked earnestly as he pulled me back to stare into my eyes.

"I didn't, but I held out hope. Plus, I presented you the perfect window to do so, with enough chaos to slip in and out easily," I responded.

"Hope? That's a dangerous and usually fatal mistake in our line of work."

"How did you know it was me and not Marie?' I blurted.

"She can understand things. Marie can't talk and doesn't hear, but she can see. When she would sit on the balcony, she would twist her wedding band on her hand as a private signal to me. She always knew I'd be watching. But your disguise was so spot on I knew it couldn't be anyone else but you to pull that off. Where is my wife? Where is she now?" he questioned.

"She's with your other daughter. We are taking good care of her until we can all transport out safely. Where is Ryan? We need to move quickly."

His eyes lit up at the mention of Chanlor with a smile on his face. He had a certain ease come upon him that he surely hadn't had in a while.

"She's dressed up as one of those crazy romance groupies out front. She's waiting on word from me."

"Tell her to find and approach the two officers handling the dogs. They'll take her from there to meet up with us."

"I hope your exfil plan is better than just 'hope'," he stated with a grin.

"Now brother, don't doubt your older sis," I smiled back.

"For the record, it was two minutes by all accounts."

"Again, don't doubt your older sis. Just saying," I chided as I walked toward the other room to grab my gear to relay to others. "Packaged is confirmed. Steve and Tom - Ryan will be on her way to you. Meet on rooftop, pronto. B, we'll be waiting for you and the flyover."

I found myself hopeful again as I grabbed my things while he inspected the apartment to see if anything additional needed to be taken. After surveying the room quickly, he realized there was nothing that was personal or of value. We both abandoned our disguises and for the first time, I finally was able to see my brother. The features we shared were remarkable; the inherit traits undeniable. This was my blood.

Tom and Steve identified Ryan and dispatched that they were making their way to the elevators in the main lobby. David and I took the stairs to gain entrance to the rooftop.

"Freddy/Jake, status on our unfriendlies…"

"They are bugging out quickly. Too much activity for them to take the risk. Looks like the diversion was a success," Jake responded first.

"Freddy, scope out and ensure they aren't leaving any surprises. Give the Birds the countdown," I instructed.

David and I were hunkered down as we approached Jake on the opposite side of the rooftop. Jake extended his hand to introduce himself and said, "Requesting to shake the hand of the brother of the bravest woman I've ever met." *Ahh shit, not now Jake.*

David's eyes furrowed and then he shook his hand likewise, "Thanks for having all our backs and for taking care of my baby girl. I hope you haven't been immersing her with those old cheesy movie quotes though. She's a tad younger than you, I doubt she's seen *Armageddon* with Bruce Willis." *Oh, this is SO my brother.*

Jake stiffened up understanding that David had had eyes on him and us this whole time. He simply responded with a "No, sir."

The three of us were prone to the ground and continued hushed conversations as we waited for the others to arrive. Tom, Steve, and Ryan and the pooches appeared and gathered with us as we patiently waited. Jake was back in position with the 338 sighting the horizon for any possible stragglers.

Freddy came over comms, "Hold onto your hats. It's about to get breezy."

A deafening noise was looming. You could feel movement. Your senses were awakening unlike any other experience. Everyone from the rooftop to down below instinctively looked up as six F-16 fighter jets flew overhead with precision and professionalism. Welcome to the brave world of the US Airforce Thunderbirds.

Performing over thirty maneuvers, they would be entertaining our crowd with a stellar, unforgettable performance while giving cover to our imminent departure.

As the fighter jets performed their miracles of feat to the northeast side, Bethany maneuvered in from the southwest almost stealth like in a Sikorsky UH-60 Black Hawk helicopter. Providing assault, aeromedical, evacuation, special operations, and cargo lift, we had the perfect vehicle for any situation. Advanced weapon systems allowed Bethany to identify and engage in static or moving targets with firing guns, rockets, or laser missiles.

David turned to me, impressed, "Nice touch. Must be nice to have friends in high places."

"I told you to trust me on this."

"I haven't trusted anyone in a long time," he stated straight-faced.

Foregoing a fast rope insertion, the UH-60 needs a one hundred-by-one-hundred space to safely land, as the main rotors tilt down at the nose of the craft. This happens to the be the same dimension requirements for air medical ambulance helicopters that many retirement and advanced facilities must have to transport patients in critical care to hospitals.

Tom was looking at me and seeing the smile I had, knowing that I finally had a missing piece of my life. I winked, indicating my appreciation for the moment and that I was able to share it with my husband. Steve helped Ryan aboard, followed by Tom and the dogs. David looked at me and said, "Age before beauty," to which I casually responded, "Well, I can't board twice."

Out of nowhere, Koda and Bruiser started barking ferociously, signaling imminent danger. Dogs can hear sounds up to a mile away. I crouched instinctively as I was nearing the rear siding main door. I then felt the *whoosh* of two sniper shots whiz past. The dogs had already jumped on David, leveling him to the ground. Jake intuitively repositioned the 338 to the direction of the shots fired. My heart raced. *He trusted me. Defcon II*

"Freddy, what the HELL!" I shouted over comms.

Freddy was barking coordinates to Jake, who was now locking in on the target. Our obviously trained sniper miscalculated due to the necessity to angle up the height of the twelve stories, speed of rotors, and the active vibration control emitted from the UH-60 that skewed their shots ever so slightly, hitting instead the armored fuselage versus one of us. Thank God for these dogs. Again. The fact the UH-60 can survive direct hits up to 23mm shells was just a serendipitous bonus.

Fortuitously for us, Jake would be taking a down shot and would not have the same obstacles impeding his shot. If it wasn't me taking the shot, Jake was the next best on the team. The 338 is also one of the quietest sniper rifles with an effective firing range of eighteen hundred meters. *Don't kid yourself, you can still hear it. It's not like the movies.* If he missed, Bethany would blow them to kingdom come.

Jake was precision-predicting on our running target and our lone survivor was no longer. *Sayonara, fucker.*

"Freddy, confirm lone mark. I repeat, confirm."

"They knew we were here. Went for glory shot when they jammed us, and we momentarily lost link."

"Contact Sedlin or Long and tell them to send outside operatives to retrieve and ID on the down low. We need verification of which contract group was sent. The recovered round I'm looking at doesn't look Russian. But who knows, they all can use the same ammo."

I turned to David. "Let's try this again. After you this time."

Ready for immediate departure, I turned to see the pristine airmanship of the Thunderbirds still going, and hoped the residents of the facility were in as much delight and awe to spark a little hope and faith.

# FORTY-TWO

TRUST ME: being a trained operative doesn't mean we don't experience elevated heart rates. The last week, much less the last twelve hours, I had been in hiding to meet a long-lost brother, almost got us both shot, and was now preparing for a coup and permanent departure. I may be morphing into something, but I am human.

Bethany flew us to Randolph Air Force Base, which is located just on the northeast side of San Antonio in Universal City, Texas.

With exquisite Spanish Colonial Revival architecture throughout the base, the base is often referred to as the "Showplace of Air Force" (or to military personnel, "The Taj"). What is not a common everyday feature on the base is the arrival of a UH-60. Typically, you'd see T-38C Talon, T-6A and T-1A's stationed. Being part of the Joint Base since 2010, aircraft from other military operations would fly in as the base does have two control towers. That second tower, would be receiving another arrival shortly that would have no transfer logs, make no headlines, and would have a limited, discreet crew operating under the strictest and highest clearance.

I think we were all still reflecting on the fact we'd made it out with only one casualty. That, and we were all together for the first time.

We had a little over an hour before our other arrivals. We were quietly escorted to the administration building and all its opulence, certainly earning its name of "The Taj." I made a mental note of the exquisite granite terrazzo floors and stairways as we were accompanied to the offices on the second floor. Looking out the windows with dusk finally arriving, the skyline of Texas once again captured my heart with brilliant shades of red, orange, and yellow, mixed with the vibrant blue Texas skies. There's a reason why they say, "it's not a state, but a state of mind." I also knew it would be my last time to step foot in this state for a long while, and felt the weight of it all.

Tom entered the room and joined me, grabbing my hand as we continued to look out at the view. "I prefer the Colorado mountains, but I must admit, I'm going to miss this view, as well."

I felt suddenly suffocated by the weight of the looming decisions and direction. "Are we doing the right thing?" I asked in earnest.

He turned his head to me. "We're making the best decisions for our family based on the information we have today. That's all we can do."

"It isn't just us, though. We're asking others to make decisions that impact their lives, as well."

"They know the same as us, and are ultimately accountable for their own decisions. You're not putting a gun to their head. You may not like what they choose, but you're going to have to trust and let go."

Trust: a word that is often mistakenly interchangeable with the word 'faith'. Trust is a belief in the reliability of truth, or in the ability of someone or something based on experience. My brother mentioned he didn't trust me; nor should he. We had no mutual experiences outside of birth. I was asking him to decide based on blind faith.

"Thank you, babe, those were the words I needed to hear. Your timing was perfect as always. I need to speak to David and his daughters. They need to make the best decisions for their own family."

"Not sure I can take credit on timing," he said with a smile, "but go do what you need to do babe. They should all be here soon."

I walked over to the other office where Ryan and David had congregated, catching up, anxiously awaiting the arrival of Chanlor and Marie. Their heads turned as I walked in, and I asked if I might intrude for a moment and speak to David privately. Ryan had a concerned look on her face. I promised I would return him to her promptly and this would only take a second. We walked out to the hallway.

"I take this is a moment of truth," he said, with his eyes smiling, the noticeable fine wrinkles on the side. Could pass for a mirage image of mine, minus the injections.

I stalled. "Well, it's the moment you make a lasting decision for you and/or your family, and I think you need to know what's about to go down to make a fully informed decision."

"Sounds pretty serious." The twinkle in his eyes now diminished into a more subdued look.

"Let me start by saying that I wasn't always looking for you and Renat, even once I learned of your existence. Self-absorbed in my own life and circumstances, I didn't understand the full impact until I had my own children in life. To me, family is everything and I was missing the beginning pieces. Often feeling a hole and abandonment, I was driven by our circumstances, but lied to myself by thinking it didn't mold me. It's who I am today."

"Partially, in truth. Past actions and experiences shape us: what you do with that, defines you. I always wondered what our given names really would have been, don't you?"

"Touché. I stand corrected and yes, I always thought of myself being named Taylor or anything else than Matti with an 'I'." I laughed and continued, "David fits you though. I could picture Mom naming you David."

"Now Renat, Jardani, got the raw end of the deal," I said jokingly. "I think maybe he would have been 'John.'"

"Outside of Shanghai, did your paths ever cross?" he asked.

"No, and you?"

"Like you, I had my own missions, then family and prevailing circumstances. I often wondered though. I still do," he said with remorse.

"Marie and Chanlor should be arriving within minutes. Let me tell you my family's plan so you can discuss with your family and adjust accordingly…"

His eyes narrowed and widened as I described in detail the forthcoming prepared actions. When it was all said and done, he looked at me and said, "You've given me quite a lot to think about. How much time do I have?"

The weight was visibly on my shoulders as I took him by the elbow and steered him to the hallway window. I pointed to the approaching HUMVEEs. "Some are coming up the drive now. We'll be out of here by midnight. You'll need to make your decision by then."

The term 'Shock and awe' (or technically known as 'speed and dominance') was coined specifically by the US military for the strategy of an overwhelming power and force to paralyze the enemy's will to fight. I was prepared to take a military term and launch it into the public sector.

I embraced David and kissed him on his cheek then left; leaving him to make his own decision. I walked down the elaborate staircase towards the entrance door with Michael Jackson, *Man in the Mirror* running through my mind… *I'm gonna make a change, For once in my life, It's gonna feel real good, Gonna make a difference, Gonna make it right…*

# FORTY-THREE

JAKE, STEVE, AND BETHANY, along with Tom and the dogs, saw the caravan and had already headed out the main doors to meet our incoming peeps. I joined Tom, Koda, and Bruiser as we anxiously awaited with excitement building inside. David and Ryan came down just in time for the vehicles to come to a stop.

I was a little surprised by the three individual drivers in the driver's seats of each vehicle. Not that they weren't completely capable of driving – I just had anticipated different people. Matthew, Mary, and Mark exited the driver's side doors, and could each be heard exclaiming a similar version of, "you won't believe the shit we've gone through to get here…"

Tom and I ran up to greet them while the others went to the passenger side to open the doors for our other travelers. One by one, we saw them passed out or nearly passed out in the vehicles. The dogs (Scout, Trooper and new addition Scully) jumped out excitedly to be greeted by Koda and Bruiser. Our seven scientists could barely walk when they escorted them out, and they stumbled onto a face plant in the courtyard. The last ones to exit the vehicles were Ainsworth and Larkin, who were completely wasted and swaying. *Dazed and Confused had nothing on them.*

I approached Ainsworth, grabbing his arm while asking, "What the hell? What happened?"

In a broken garble, I think he responded with, "You told us to show them normalcy…and we did…Marine style. Introduced them to Jameson. I think they like Fireball, too." He ended that in a hyena type laugh before bending himself over in a hysterical fit, looking for a non-existent cigarette.

I looked to Larkin, "I told you both to take them out - hell, play kickball," I exclaimed exasperated.

Larkin, looking no better than Ainsworth approached smiling a fool's grin. His head was now shaved bald, adding to the element of surprise. "Ms. Matti, we had a…we had a …we had a helluva time. These guys are great. I mean…we can't understand a fucking thing they said, like not one word…but there might be something in them after all. I think they can pull off this miracle."

I looked towards Tom, Jake, Steve and Bethany and we all just laughed. The kids not so much. David and Ryan didn't know what to think.

"Help me out. Get these clowns inside and get them cleaned up and ready," I said mischievously.

Bethany gave me that look. "Easier if we just knock them out for it," she said before herding the drunk idiots with Jake and Steve's help and having them line up like preschoolers as they were escorted back in. Ainsworth and Larkin were attempting to sing the Marine Hymn and could be heard singing, "We fight our country's battles, in the air, on land, and sea." Only thing more comical than their singing was the non-English-speaking scientists trying to join in.

Scout and Trooper were rolling in the grass. Scully was asleep, or possibly passed out. Koda and Bruiser were nipping at their heels to get them all up and in line. *What a spectacle this must have been to any other witnesses. And we're the best of the best. Good lord.*

While still outside, the last vehicle we had expected to arrive was coming down to greet us. I looked to David and smiled; this one was for him.

Freddy pulled up in a black, custom passenger van. There was no one in the passenger seat beside him, but you could see two heads behind him. David walked up to the sliding door, he looked back at me and smiled, and then opened the door to his remaining family. Tears filled his eyes and ran down his cheeks.

Freddy came over to join us and I grabbed Tom and kids and whispered, "Let's leave them be. Come with me."

# FORTY-FOUR

---

TOM AND I HAD DISCUSSED the probabilities of each scenario and outcome to determine what best to do for our family. We were torn over what to do. Even though we still see them as children (ok, me more so than Tom), they aren't really children anymore, are they? They were forging their own paths, so we decided to present options and risks to them, as it was the right thing to do. It was their lives we were asking to modify the course of, for the sake of protecting America and our family, at all costs.

After exploring options, it was them that gently reminded us...United we stand, divided we fall. Human nature would prevail again. To fight, freeze or flee. Our children choose family, and they choose to fight. With their youthful experience, they provided us an alternative we hadn't really considered as an option. Our family was more than just the four of us. It was Freddy, Bethany, Jake, Steve, and even Ainsworth and Larkin (and of course the four, now five, pups).

Now, we had more to consider with David, Marie, Ryan and Chanlor. The kids were the ones that urged us to take the scientists with us, too. Not just for their protection, but in hopes that, with encouragement versus fear, that maybe they could unlock the mysteries of my creation and this mutating virus.

Freddy, my non-biological father, and former commander had his arm around me in a fatherly gesture as we all walked back into the building. At last, I had everyone I needed and wanted together …but I knew it was time to say good-bye.

Tom took the kids to go search for something to eat and drink while Freddy and I sat around a desk talking through events. Freddy was always my hidden protector. *How could I ever repay him?*

"How did David take it when you explained your plans?" he inquired.

"About what I thought. He's been through hell. Just like all of us, I guess. I'm sure it's asking a lot for him, either way he chooses. United or divided, time will soon tell," I said as I continued to look out the office window.

"What's your gut telling you?" he asked as he folded his hands together on his lap.

"How proficient are you still in flying?"

"What's with the deflecting?" he replied.

"Not deflecting, mentally calculating. You can still operate?"

"Can I still operate? I'm not that old, and I taught you a thing or two, if memory recalls," he said with a sharp grin.

"So, then, that would be a yes. That's good, that's what I was counting on."

"Where's this going, Matti?"

"When the time comes, you'll need to take the Blackhawk and fly David and his family to the destination of their choice. After that, I need you to go back to Denver, then to Ft. Bragg to join up with the others." I had turned to face him now.

"You don't think he's going to join us?"

"Call it women's intuition, or triplet telepathy, but no. He's going to take his family another direction and I understand why."

"I think you're right. I'll bite then: what's back in Denver that we need first?

With a tenderness in my eyes and a sadness in my heart, I replied, "It's time for you to go home, Freddy. Go get that girl Erika."

I wasn't sure what I witnessed in his emotions.... understanding, sadness, fear, or maybe all of them mixed.

He looked out the window and just stared before answering, "What if she doesn't want the same?"

Fear of rejection is a powerful factor based on past experiences. His entire life, he felt rejected by my mother, overcoming loneliness, depression, self-criticism by overcompensating when it came to me and even my brothers.

"Then, I'll know where to pick you up, and you're no worse off. The question is whether or not you're perfect for each other," I said with a forced smile.

"Should have known you'd ruin this moment with a quote from *Good Will Hunting*," he genuinely laughed.

I got up from my chair and walked over to hug him still sitting in his chair. We just sat there while I cradled his head. My desire to not let go, conflicted with wanting him to leave. Tears were silently streaming down both our faces.

"Go get her Freddy, and then join Tia, Aldo, and my parents and start your next chapter. They're all waiting for you." I whispered.

We were startled out of our trance when Bethany entered the room. "Matti, there's a secure call for you in the other office."

Freddy and I embraced once more before I let go to move towards the door. I turned back at the doorway to look at him, eyes swollen. "You good?" I asked.

"I guess I need to get ready. I have to go see about a girl," he replied.

My smile widened ever so slightly at the movie reference, "Atta boy," I said, and I left for the other office.

# FORTY-FIVE

"I WAS BRIEFED that you had a successful exfil - only one casualty. Not like you," he started the conversation.

"Getting kinder in my old age, plus...I serve at the pleasure of the President," I responded.

He laughed at that before continuing, "I know you haven't filled me in on the exact details, Matti. You've made some big asks. I need to understand if lives will be lost because of what you'll do."

"Mr. President...Easton...No sir, I'll be saving lives because of what they've done. As we've discussed, for your own safety and protection, the less you know, the better, but I will need you to react swiftly when the time comes. I'll be creating a short-term issue to drive long-term results. You have less than two years on your term. Get to it, as they say."

"You've made some powerful enemies."

"Easton, when this is all done, history will either label me a destroyer or a savior. I believe you are a praying man, so let's pray that it's the latter." I paused for effect before adding, "Is my special delivery on the way?"

"Yes, I even had it specially painted for you. I think you'll like it. Intrator is bringing it, like you asked so as not to raise any eyebrows. ETA one hour. What made you change your mind on him?"

"I hoped you sent it stocked," I quantified, to his first statement. "As for Intrator, he's not running for office after this. If he was involved, he would have wanted to stay in position of power. Of course, I could claim that anyone wanting to run for any government office has to be a little mentally unstable." I ended sarcastically, "But, we also drilled down through mounds of records and saw where he was being infiltrated as a setup."

"I think we're all on 'mentally unstable.' Anything else I can do for you?" he asked.

"Personally, I'm an advocate for age limits for anyone assuming the role of the President. Maybe you can get that passed before you go?"

"Hey, now," he teased. "Sadly, you are right." Turning to a more serious tone, he ended, "Matti, it's been our honor and our privilege. Godspeed."

"I will always continue to serve. God willing, Mr. President, God willing."

# FORTY-SIX

TOM AND THE BOYS had scored some serious snacks and beverages, and everyone was congregated in the acting commander's office. The mood was relatively lighthearted with banter from all of us telling stories. Each person trying to one up the other.

Although all were now briefed on the next mission, I had left out one element of surprise that was about to hit. I asked everyone to gather to the north window and pointed to distant lights in the night sky that were approaching.

Bethany, with eyes practically tearing, asked, "Is that a new G7 coming towards us?"

"Oh, B. You must think bigger." *She's going to flip.*

All were scratching their heads, wondering what this could be and trying to get a better angle to see.

There are only a handful of aircraft that are as famous or recognized as the one that would be landing. Even though this aircraft was built over thirty years ago, it was retrofitted and rebuilt to be the best of the best. And now, it was being sent off to retirement and had found a new home.

A little unknown fact for the American public: it's always wiser to build in two. Hell, we even learned this from the fictional billionaire Hadden in the movie *Contact*.

In the dark of the night, looming towards us and now painted in a matte black, was Air Force One, a VC-25A, created from a highly modified Boeing 747-200 series. Two new replacements had been in production and came in. *Fortunate timing for us. Another miracle.* Typically, a retired plane would go to a Presidential Gallery. Since the public is unaware that there are always two planes, one will go to the Gallery, and we were now the proud owners of the other. I didn't pay a penny for it. Reminded them it was for services rendered. *(I had career-ending dossiers on all of them...)*

The amenity we needed most for the time being was the extensive and advanced electronic system. With over four thousand interior square feet, we had ample room between the twenty-two of us (including dogs). The plane commonly accommodates seventy. The plane isn't equipped with any weapons (we'll rectify that), but has jamming radar, ejecting flares and can withstand the electromagnetic pulse from a nuclear blast. *Might be useful if China and Taiwan tensions ramp up higher. Just saying.*

The excitement in the air was building with talk about how I'd managed this without their knowledge. I walked over to David and asked, "Will you be joining us in taking our new transportation to a new home?"

I already knew his answer, but it was time to hear it.

"Thank you - really, thank you, Matti. I hope your country knows everything you have sacrificed for them. Your offer is very generous, but the girls are going with their mom and me. We are looking to escape with new identities and find a permanent home. Under different circumstances, we would have taken you up on it. We can't afford the risk of them trying to track the both of us

166

together, so we think it's better for all of us, if you and I were separated. I wish…I wish…we could have been together this whole time. I always missed having siblings." *It emerged that David preferred Julius Caesar's divide and conquer approach, while I chose Sun Tzu, to be united.*

"I figured as much. I do understand and respect. Do you know where you will go? Freddy will escort you to wherever you want. He, too, is choosing new direction for love. It looks like we have all sacrificed for that," I said with a genuine admiration.

"I have one last hurrah, so to speak, before we can start our new lives. I have a special Mexican delivery for Michaels."

"Ha, he might not need it after what's about to drop, but it doesn't hurt to have a backup." Continuing, I said, "We both need to focus on the impacts of our creation and what's at stake. I'll keep you posted on any new developments." I extended my hand to shake and brought him in for a long embrace. "If you need anything, anything at all…a toothpick even…you know how to find me."

With an emotional response, he simply said, "Thank you sister. Ditto."

# FORTY-SEVEN

WE HAD A LIMITED TURNAROUND time to get this plane and the Blackhawk up in the air. As we approached, we noticed there was a little something extra that President Borrelli had painted on the tail assembly. In all its splendid glory, a bald eagle was the new emblem of our fine craft. It was an unmistakable sign. A sign we were on the right path. *There are signs everywhere.*

Intrator approached me and shook my hand. "It's a pleasure to finally meet The Matti Baker. Thank you for believing in me. I'm glad I wasn't one of your many distinguished targets."

"I took emotion out and followed the facts, sir. Plain and simple. I drilled down deep enough to determine who was trying to frame you. When someone tells you something once, you can dismiss it. When someone tells you repeatedly, then that's on you."

"Our friends in China and Russia. How can I help Easton?" he asked solemnly.

"You swore an oath to support and defend the Constitution of the United States, against all enemies, foreign and domestic. Work inside out and do your job, sir. Help Borrelli while you two are still in office. It's time to clean house, so to speak."

"We thank you for your service, Matti, and I thank you for your perseverance and loyalty," he said, with a slight bow showing respect.

Intrator was then quickly whisked off the base, and afterwards the rest of us collectively hugged and kissed everyone good-bye. I was worried about Jake and Chanlor, but this was right decision based on current circumstances. I worried about the kids missing Freddy, but they could still reach out. I worried about Steve, Bethany, Ainsworth, Larkin and seven people who didn't speak our language. All of them had lost their families; we were the only family they knew. We reminded ourselves that this was not the end, just the beginning of the next chapter. Eventually, we knew we all had to let go to move forward.

We boarded the still somewhat inebriated scientists, Ainsworth, and Larkin, onto the aircraft. No longer singing, they looked more like death warmed over. Bethany dosed them all up and they now looked like passengers in sleep pods in their reclined chairs. They'd be out for a hot minute.

Tom, Jake, Steve, the kids, and the dogs were next to board and in were in high spirits as they explored the new vast amenities of the plane. Bethany was talking to Freddy, saying their final good-byes before she entered the cockpit.

Just Freddy and I were alone outside. My eyes were welling up again, my heart was breaking. He hugged me one last time before saying, "If it doesn't work out, I'll be needing a ride. Maybe I can convince her to join our circus."

"Freddy, listen to me. If she does want to join…RUN!"

"I love you, kiddo. Whatever you have inside you, your desire to protect and prevail is always stronger. You were created for a higher purpose. I've always believed in you. Get those scientists to work that miracle. You got this." He kissed me on the head, and with that, he turned towards David and the others and started his new journey. *Miracles are not what we don't understand, but what is done for us that we can't do ourselves. Only one person can do that.*

I watched until they were all boarded and the start of the rotors whirled. With my hair blowing, my hand was high in the air, gently waving good-bye until they could no longer be seen. Slowly, I joined Bethany in the cockpit.

"It's just you and I, in here. About to do some *Thelma and Louise* bullshit with countless others," she started in. *God, I loved my best friend.*

"You know, I was thinking it's more like that movie, *Transcendence*, with Johnny Depp. Remember that one?" I asked.

"That one escapes me. You typically have us watch movies from the eighties. Repeatedly, I might add." This said as she was fiddling with equipment.

"Oh, hell, you fall asleep within ten minutes of any movie anyways, but you remember this one. There's this virus, it wipes everything out, yadda, yadda, yadda," I added.

"Oh great, hell. Just say hell," as she continued to flip switches.

Tom came up to the cockpit to check on me and whispered, "You ok, babe?" *My love.*

Bethany, not missing a beat, said, "You know I can hear you. Just saying. Your plus one is right here. Always."

Laughing, we all needed the release. I turned to Tom, "Thanks, babe. All good. Will you go tell Steve to send us off with a good one, and tell the kids I'll be down after we get situated?" I mouthed to him silently, "love you," as he exited for down below.

Bethany turned to me. "All systems a go. You ready?"

"One sec…I need to send a heads up to our friend Jackson. The Operation Eagle Eye countdown has started. Countdown four hours…There, message sent. Your co-pilot is now at your service…"

"Who knew your secret talent that emerged over this mutating virus would be computer hacking, right?"

"I know, right? What can I say. I'm special."

"Oh, you are special, alright." Her whop-eye slanted, "Hope you're buckled in. Jake better be bringing up some popcorn to get this party started," she said as she throttled down the runway. I was praying she wasn't going to try to max speed it on take-off. I wouldn't put it past her.

Over the speakers, we heard Steve put on Garth Brooks,

New Way to Fly…*And the tears that they cry, Now the lesson's been learned, They've all crashed and burned, But they can leave it behind, If they could just find, A new way to fly…*

# FORTY-EIGHT

## 3.2.1. Defcon

OPERATION EAGLE EYE launched in the early morning, while most American's were asleep. A form of resurrection coming to terms, to bring to view and cast attention on the just and unjust. Surely it was a sign that we were on the right path.

The preliminary effects would be felt by only a select few when the markets opened. *Well, if they opened...*

There was a silent ignorance on one of the highest risks to all people with the escalation of cyber-attacks standing out amongst all other top global concerns. You can put climate change on the back burner. *Just saying.*

Ransomware was getting all the hot action and it wasn't biased attacks. Remember what China was focusing on...

These attacks don't discriminate. Big, small, rich, poor, individuals, or businesses – it didn't matter what color or sex, they attacked them all. ***There is one quality that is unique to the human species: regardless of race, color, gender. It's when harm is known and done anyways in response to a financial benefit... GREED.***

Reminded me of that YouTube skit... *Honey badger don't care. Honey badger don't give a shit...* It was time to eliminate some honey badgers.

We were over the Caribbean Sea when the first news reports started flooding in on catastrophic cyber-attacks. DEFCON had started.

Our dear pal, Jackson, had the exclusive story thanks to our secure intel, and was one tweeting individual…

**Tam Jackson**　　　　**100.1M followers**　　　　**1 day**
@Truthwillsetyoufree
HOLY $! Carter Michaels personal, business, & offshore accts have been hacked leaving ZERO net worth! That's Billions gone with a cap "B"

---

**LIKES AND RETWEETS HAVE BEEN TURNED OFF ON THIS ACCOUNT.**

---

**Tam Jackson**　　　　**101.4M followers**　　　　**23hrs**
@Truthwillsetyoufree
Several key congress members & SPEAKER OF HOUSE also affected by cyber-attack!! Again, ZERO.

**Tam Jackson**　　　　**102.4M followers**　　　　**22hrs**
@Truthwillsetyoufree
ALL markets are closed before opening bell due to cyber security concerns! 1st time since 2020!!

**Tam Jackson**　　　　**102.7 followers**　　　　**21hrs**
@Truthwillsetyoufree
How do you get congress to react quickly? Asking for a friend. Payback is a bitch.

**Tam Jackson**               **103.2M followers**               **20hrs**
@Truthwillsetyoufree
Epic meltdown on all levels. Well, at Congress.

**Tam Jackson**               **104.1M followers**               **16hrs**
@Truthwillsetyoufree
News channels have been banned from congressional oversight committees. Land of the Free unless it involves congress.

**Tam Jackson**               **104.4M followers**               **12hrs**
@Truthwillsetyoufree
Borrelli addresses cyber-attacks. China and Russia being investigated, but confirms it's an inside job. Can we address Big Pharma and rising insurance issues now?

**Tam Jackson**               **105.6M followers**               **10hr**
@Truthwillsetyoufree
Will markets be closed tmrw? Stay tuned and get the TRUTH here!

**Tam Jackson**               **105.9M followers**               **10hrs**
@Truthwillsetyoufree
JUST CONFIRMED. Several NFL owners account have been hacked as well. Bet we see some action now!

**Tam Jackson**               **116.3M followers**               **9hrs**
@Truthwillsetyoufree
Reports of Michaels being rushed to hospital. Not heart attack.

| Tam Jackson | 116.7M followers | 4hrs |

@Truthwillsetyoufree

Michaels confirmed dead. Alleged to be a pill his Co manufactures laced with a specific Mexican-based fentanyl.

| Tam Jackson | 118.1M followers | 3hrs |

@Truthwillsetyoufree

HUGE anonymous donation received by AFSP, Wounded Warriors, and First Nations. Market still closed.

| Tam Jackson | 129.1M followers | 1hr |

@Truthwillsetyoufree

---

**THIS ACCOUNT HAS BEEN BLOCKED FOR VIOLATING TERMS OF AGREEMRNT.**

---

I reflected on the thirteenth century poet, Rumi: "Greed makes man blind and foolish and makes him an easy prey for death." We had entered a new age of DEFCON, an attack on the nucleus of society and a far greater threat than any weaponry attack. Maybe I did have a higher purpose in my creation? There are signs everywhere. *If you read them.*

On autopilot to our new destination, we were all dancing in the aisles as Steve had a new playlist going, starting with Prince's

*Let's Go Crazy...Dearly beloved...But I'm here to tell you there's something else; the afterworld, A world of never-ending happiness, You can always see the sun, day or night...*

## NOTE FROM THE AUTHOR

That was fun, right?

I'm not sure what genre to put this in. Part of my dilemma when marketing. It has Action, Suspense, Thriller, Humor, Religious, Military, Conspiracy, Psychological, and Political overtones. (Ok, there's not much Romance. I'd need a ghostwriter for that).

I love all the greats: Patterson, Flynn, Woods, Thor, Childs, Clancy, but my thriller series isn't like them. I mean, who doesn't love a charming protagonist with tons of resources? Sign me up! So, I created a new version intertwining current and historical events and conspiracies. I hope I gave you some things to think about (or at least investigate on your own). *Just saying*. Plus, I give you Spotify and movie playlists. (Bonus. I mean, really).

I do come from a long line of military. My grandfather was a Prisoner of War in WWII, my Dad was army intelligence, Uncle killed in Vietnam, Brother was former Vice Chief of AF, other Brother formerly in AF, a slew of other cousins in military, and my eldest son is in the Space Force. That's why this series lends to a patriotic theme. Plus, I strongly believe it makes us a stronger nation if we're united.

I wish I could show you the first chapter to the next book, BAKER.

I can't. It's not written, but it's been in my head for four long years and was what started all this storytelling in the first place. To many readers' surprise, I always read the last chapter of a book first. (Don't hate me.) I want to know how the author gets there and if I would have done the same. Well, BAKER is my beginning. I will give you a hint: All characters in this series are based on real people in my life, except one. Oh my, that's all I can share.

Thanks for hanging with me as I navigate this writing industry.

I promise you, with BAKER, you will either think I'm crazy or brilliant…maybe both…so get your drink on and get ready for one hell of a ride!

Carpe diem,

-MP

*Did you know that when you leave a (great) review,*
*it usually gets featured in the next book and/or on my website?*
*Go to Goodreads or Amazon to post.*
**(Really, go there NOW and do it!)**

*Didn't enjoy it? Well, leave a review anyways and thank you for*
*the small contribution towards my retirement.*

Print and digital books can be purchased on my website
or Amazon, B&N, Kobo or Apple books.

| | |
|---|---|
| American Book Festival | 2019 Finalist |
| Independent Author Award | 2019 Finalist |
| Pencraft | 2019 1$^{st}$ Place |
| Eric Hoffer Awards | 2020 Finalist |
| Writer's Digest | 2021 Honorable Mention |
| Pencraft | 2022 Runner-Up |
| BestThriller.com | 2022 Finalist |

**www.michelepackard.com**

Award-winning author, Michele Packard, comes from a military family and worked as a cable tv executive before staying at home to raise her three children. She has written in both the fiction and non-fiction genres, utilizing her experiences and wit to share stories with others. Her family calls her "AESOP" as she tends to exaggerate (a lot).

She is a frequent traveler with her husband and is the primary caretaker of the family's beloved two labs.

Instagram:@aesopstories

Goodreads:@michelepackard

https://www.bookbub.com/profile/michele-packard

## Books by Packard
AESOP
FABLE
TELLER
COUNTERINTELLIGENCE
DEFCON
BAKER – TBA

Non-Fiction:
Scoochie-Scoochie Nite-Nite
Willed Ignorance - 2023

*Be afraid, be very afraid.*

# DEFCON
## SPOTIFY LIST

BERLIOZ - SYMPHONIE FANTASTIQUE 5TH MOVEMENT
BILLIE EILISH - NO TIME TO DIE
BUTTHOLE SURFERSS - PEPPER
DON MCLEAN - AMERICAN PIE
GARTH BROOKS - NEW WAY TO FLY
JAY Z/JUSTIN TIMBERLAKE - HOLY GRAIL
JOHN DENVER - LEAVING ON A JET PLANE
JOHN WAITE - CHANGE
KANSAS - DUST IN THE WIND
MICHAEL JACKSON - MAN IN THE MIRROR
OUTSKIRTS- LET'S DO THIS
OZZY OSBOURNE - SEE YOU ON THE OTHER SIDE
PINK - WILD HEDARTS CAN'T BE BROKEN
PRINCE - LET'S GO CRAZY
RAGE AGAINST MACHINE - KILLING IN THE NAME
ROBERT PALMER - ADDICTED TO LOVE
SARAH MCLAUGHLIN - POSSESSION
STEVE MILLER BAND -FLY LIKE AN EAGLE

# DEFCON
## MOVIE & TV SHOW LIST

A FEW GOOD MEN
AIR FORCE ONE
ARMAGEDDON
BOSCH
BOURNE LEGACY
BRUCE LMIGHTY
COCKTAIL
DAZED AND CONFUSED
DIE HARD
FRIDAY NIGHT LIGHTS
GOOD WILL HUNTING
JOHN WICK
KINGHT AND DAY
MANCHURIAN CANDIDATE
MI-III
PACIFIC RIM

PEAKY BLINDERS
PHENOMENON
POINT BREAK
ROCKY III
SLEEPING WITH THE ENEMY
SPEED
TANGO AND CASH
TEMPLE OF DOOM
THE BONE COLLECTOR
THE DA VINCI CODE
THE DEVIL'S ADVOCATE
THE GRAY MAN
THE SAINT
THELMA AND LOUISE
TOOTSIE
TOP GUN/MAVERICK
TRANSCENDENCE
WRATH OF KHAN

Made in the USA
Monee, IL
18 May 2023

34032456R00114